THE
GOOD
FIGHT

BOOK ONE OF THE LAST ENEMY SERIES

by

DAN E. HENDRICKSON

ISBN: 9781734518703

Last Enemy series:

Book one: *The Good Fight*

Book two: *The Cartel Crusher*

Book three: *The Last Enemy*

More books to follow:

The Legend of Deputy Jim

The Commander

DEDICATION

This first book is dedicated to my Corps brother Keith Jackson. Keith, the writing break you gave me a couple of years ago gave me the confidence to take this one on. Sure love you brother!

THANK YOU

As any first-time author comes to find out, writing and publishing a book is very much a team effort. First and foremost, I want to thank God Almighty Who worked with me and put great people in my life to help me put this story into writing. Second, I want to thank my wife Cheryl for supporting me and proofreading my initial manuscript. She was a real trooper and inspired me all the way. Third, my daughter Rebeccah for doing the initial editing before sending it on to the publisher. Thanks honey, you made a huge difference. Fourth, Susie Catlin for accepting the commission to paint a beautiful watercolor for the covers of the original series. Last of all I want to thank my editor David Navarro. This would have been very scary without him. Thanks!

CONTENTS

CHAPTER ONE

MAN OVERBOARD

Thirteen Years Ago

As the hot summer sun sets over the Texas-Mexico horizon, Commander Jacob Edwards, Captain of a United States Coast Guard *Hamilton-class* cutter, *First Responder*, stands on the dock at Station Brazos, Texas, talking to Chief Roberto Garcia, his father in-law, about his daughter, twelve-year-old Danielle and how much of a little fireball she is, always getting into trouble, and never satisfied with anything but first place.

"She's just like you and Jim," Roberto says with an exasperated but friendly chuckle, "just the girl version."

Jacob adds, "Oh, she's got her mother's artsy-crafty side. Look at all that dancing she does. I swear if I have to sit through another hour and a half of watching other people's kids perform just to see mine do something for two and a half minutes, I'll explode."

Roberto gives a big Latino sigh and says, "But you go to karate tournaments and swim meets and shout your brains out for two hours, and then Mary and Danielle have to drag you away at the end when you're telling all the coaches and instructors how you would have done it better."

"Yes, you're right," Jacob admits. "Mary loves Danielle's dancing, and I love all the rest."

"Well believe me, Jacob, I have raised three boys and one girl, and you have to spread yourself thin to support everything but it's worth it," Roberto says. He clears his throat and wipes the beginning of a tear from his eye. "I apologize, Jacob. I refuse to think that my little girl is never going to have another child."

Jacob puts a reassuring hand on his father-in-law's shoulder, "It's okay, Pops, we have accepted it and are quite content with our little spunky monkey." Jacob's radio chirps and his second-in-command, Lt. Commander Phillips, says, "Sir, we have a distress call coming from a cruise ship that just left Cozumel about forty minutes ago. They are under attack by a party of unknown assailants."

Jacob gulps, and looks at Roberto with astonishment, "What do you mean under attack, and what unknown assailants?"

"Well sir, it looks like pirates. Probably the same ones that have been harassing smaller yachts and boats farther south," says Phillips.

The questions start to fly. "Are they in international waters yet and is that ship one of ours or is it flying another flag?"

"The cruise ship belongs to a European company sir, but eighty percent of the passengers are U.S. citizens."

"Have the Mexican authorities responded yet?"

"No sir, seems to be some squabble about jurisdiction and such. What do you want to do, sir?"

Jacob throws up one hand, looks at Roberto and then answers, "What do you think? We're going to go help that ship. Get ready, and I'll handle HQ."

"You need some help, Son?" Roberto asks.

Putting his hand on Roberto's shoulder, Jacob says, "Pops, you know your whole crew is swim rescue and that ship is not even out of Mexican waters yet."

Mimicking his gesture, Roberto responds, "Well maybe some fell overboard and need our help. Besides if I let my little Mary's man go into harm's way when I could have helped, I could never look her in the eye again."

Jacob knows when to back down to his father-in-law, "Okay, Roberto, I'll think of something to justify taking you along."

Chief Roberto and Commander Edwards round up their crews and head for Jacob's United States Coast Guard *Hamilton-class* cutter. They board the 378-foot ship in what seems like milliseconds as Jacob gives the order to launch. The *First Responder* has a top speed of 29 knots, but he prays he can get at least 31 knots if he maneuvers right. Commander Jacob Edwards hates pirates and it scares the hell out of him that someone in the Gulf thinks they can take on anything as big as a cruise ship.

Petty officer John Bliss scampers up the main deck stairway to the outside front view of Jacob's ship, out of breath and completely out of his depth. "Sir, I have three sector commanders trying to contact us and all of them want to speak with you, ASAP!"

Jacob smiles a bit. Three sector commanders. A shit-storm is about to erupt. It's best to report to his sector commander only. "Give me Captain William Harrington at Corpus Christi, and you tell New Orleans and Key West to contact him in five minutes."

He grabs the com, listens to Harrington bark, then says, "Yes sir, I know how delicate this one is but they are not in international waters yet and the Mexican government is playing politics. By the way, Captain, I commandeered Chief Roberto and some of his crew to help with any water rescues."

Harrington doesn't like it. "Damn it, Jacob, you have a complement of two hundred sixty-seven with a full swim rescue unit on board."

He was ready for this, "Yes, but no one knows these waters better than Roberto, and besides, I couldn't stop him."

Will sighs. Yes, Mary's dad can be even more stubborn than his son-in-law at times, especially when it comes to family.

"Okay, don't worry; I'll smooth your requisition of personnel over somehow. You're less than one year away from becoming a full captain and probably getting one of those new security cutters when they come out, make sure you don't go off half-cocked. You run this one by the book; everyone will be watching."

"Will, if we don't respond in force, lives could be lost and we'll be the ones caught with our pants down. Those people don't have anyone else to help them. I have to overtake with extreme prejudice. Those pirates have never taken on anything like a cruise ship before. They're going to be very scared and very dangerous. Besides, if we do this right, Mexico will back us up and the brass will have nothing but a victory to brag about."

"Okay, but keep your temper in check. I know how you feel about these guys, but the whole world is watching. Overtake them, arrest them, and try not to kill anyone."

"Aye aye Captain—Edwards out."

Jacob hands the mic back to the chief. He knows he needs to tell Will soon that he's going to turn down that promotion to captain, retire, and go help his dad build the business in Manheim. It's time to give Mary and Danielle a more stable life, and he knows his parents want him and his family home. Honestly, he's just ready to go home and kick some ass in the auto auction business again.

But right now, he's got a big problem to take care of, and he hates pirates—damned despicable pirates, drugs, human trafficking, rape, smuggling, and now hijacking cruise ships. They mostly stick farther south near Central America and South Mexico, attacking little yachts, fishing boats, even a few minor port raids, but nothing like this. What the hell are they thinking now? Though not usually the praying type, Jacob decides right now it's best. "God You know me, I'm not into combat, never have been, but I can't stand to let bullies get away. Please just help me stop these guys and keep those people safe, and don't let anything happen to mine or Pop's crew. Thanks Lord."

"Amen," says Roberto as he walks up from behind. He puts a reassuring hand on his son-in-law's shoulder, ready to face down hell with this man if he has to.

The *First Responder* makes 31 knots, and no one can explain why, but Chief Roberto bows his head and says, "*Gracias A Dios.*" Under the cover of night, at approximately 11:46 p.m., Eastern Standard Time, Commander Edwards' ship storms into one of the most bizarre scenes that either he or Roberto have ever witnessed in their combined maritime experiences. Just twenty miles off the port of Cozumel, a Caribbean cruise ship is surrounded by three other ships; an older refurbished cutter, a large barge, and a small cargo ship. Each ship has what looks like multiple assailants pointing every handheld weapon imaginable at the defenseless cruise ship. On the cutter, there looks to be an old-style World War II cannon.

"Sir, there is a smaller long-range high-powered yacht docked to the Cruise ship and at least twenty armed pirates on the upper deck. It looks like there are least fifty hostages on their knees being held at gunpoint," says Lt. Commander Williams, looking through his binoculars.

Jacob looks at the situation with the practiced eye of a maritime commander who has nineteen plus years of experience on these waters. First, he has to deal with that cannon, and next, make sure those pirates on that upper deck don't kill anyone.

"We need to place ourselves between that cannon and the cruise ship," Jacob orders. It is dark on the water except for the five boats all facing one another.

Bliss comes running up the stairs again and says, "Sir, I have sector Key West on the line but it is not the sector commander, it's the Vice Commandant of the Coast Guard and he wants a word with you right now."

"I'll take it in private," he says and steps off the command deck holding the com. "Yes sir, Admiral, Commander Edwards here."

Rear Admiral James Harrington, Vice Commandant of the United States Coast Guard answers, "Edwards, you'd better be holding your dick in both hands right now because you just stormed into a diplomatic nightmare. Not only is the Mexican president blowing up the commander's and chief's phones, but so is Cuba, Belize, Guatemala, Honduras, the Cayman Islands, and Jamaica. They're all threatening some sort of retaliation if you start an international incident down there."

Jacob endeavors to hold his temper in check as he responds, "Well sir, there is the small matter of a certain cruise ship being held hostage by modern day pirates with the largest group of ships I have ever seen being used by any of those scumbags since I have had the privilege of hunting their sorry asses. Not to mention almost fifteen hundred passengers on board and about eighty percent of them are United States citizens."

Bliss sticks his head around the corner and says, "We have three long range network news choppers approaching us from Miami. They want to know if you want to make a statement."

Harrington immediately interrupts, shouting, "Don't tell them a fucking thing, Commander; I'll handle the press from here. Look Edwards, you're all alone on this one. We can't get the Navy involved until at least one of these countries asks for help. The Coast Guard does have some jurisdictional privileges granted by all these countries to protect them from stuff like this, however Mexico is being really squirrely about this one. They won't send any help, and they keep warning us to be very careful how we escalate the situation. Apparently, there's a party going on for the eighteenth birthday of the Mexican president's daughter on that ship. They picked up a bunch of VIP kids in Cozumel and we're getting calls from all over the Caribbean by scared parents asking about them. You're walking a tight rope, Commander, and we are all watching very closely."

Jacob, holding the microphone a few inches from his ear rolls his eyes and says, "Thanks for all the strategic advice sir. I am sure it will come in handy in saving everyone's—"

BLAAM! Jacob's ship reels back as if it had just run into something. He looks in the direction of the noise and sees one of the lifeboats on fire. "What the hell was that?" he yells, as another blast explodes a few yards off the side of his boat.

Lt. Commander Phillips yells back across the deck, "Mortar shells are coming off the pirate's cutter, sir. Looks like M2 Goon Guns, sir."

Harrington, frustrated, says in a loud, obnoxious, raspy voice, "What the hell is a Goon Gun, Edwards?"

Jacobs glares at the mic and says, "It's a rifled mortar weapon, sir, used in Vietnam, mainly on land but we've seen them before."

Harrington asks, not expecting an answer, "Where do they get this stuff, Edwards?"

Still looking at the mic, Jacob yells back, annoyed. "I don't know sir, maybe eBay? I have to go sir; we are under attack."

Harrington says, "Don't you hang up on me boy!" CLICK.

Jacob ends the connection and throws the com back to Bliss. He yells at his gunnery officer to crank up the OTO Melara 76 mm gun and target that cutter.

Why the hell aren't they using that cannon? he wonders. He decides that it must be fake, used to scare ships into surrendering so they can get close enough to make those Goon Guns a real threat. But Jacob knew there was nothing wrong with his cannon. The OTO Melara 76 mm was compact enough to be installed on relatively small warships and patrol boats. The gun's high rate of fire and various specialized ammunition made it well-suited for many situations and therefore was one hell of a pirate deterrent for the United States Coast Guard *Hamilton* cutter fleet. Commander Jacob Edwards would make good use of it today.

Jacob tells his second-in-command to target the rudder on that pirate cutter. He explains to Lt. Commander Phillips that he doesn't want that thing escaping, that they've just drifted out of range of those Goon Guns, and that since the pirates fired on them the Navy can now get involved, so he wants them to stay put.

"Aye aye Commander," says Phillips. He has the gunnery officer maneuver the 76 mm cannon to point directly at the ass-end of that old cutter and fire. They take a big chunk out of the stern, but miss the rudder. "Sir, the cutter is pulling away, shall we pursue?"

"Negative Phillips, they are the Navy's problem now, our priority is the cruise ship."

"Yes sir."

Roberto steps up to his son-in-law and says, "That cutter is getting out of here pretty fast, pretty souped up for a pirate refab."

"Yes," says Jacob, "there's going to be a lot of unanswered questions after this one." Just then, Jacob feels a whisk of air like a horse whip cracking by his left ear. He turns to see a bullet hole just inches from his head in the wall behind him. Roberto tackles Jacob and throws him down to the deck even as two more shots slam into the same wall just inches from one another.

"Holy shit, was that sniper fire coming from the fleeing cutter!" Phillips shouts as he dives to the deck.

Roberto looks at Jacob and says, "That cutter is at least a quarter mile away from us. Where are a bunch of Caribbean pirates going to get a world class sniper like that?"

"Yes, where indeed?" Jacob responds as he looks over at the gunnery officer who gives the all clear.

Phillips jumps up and hollers at Bliss, "You tell naval command that those bastards just tried to assassinate our skipper with very professional sniper fire!"

"Yes sir," says Bliss. "Lieutenant Commander, sir, the small speed yacht is pulling away from the cruise ship and all the pirates are leaving the hostages and running to the aft of the ship."

Jacob yells, "I want to be on that boat in five minutes Lieutenant Commander!"

"You got it, sir!" Phillips yells as he maneuvers the cutter alongside the cruise ship while Commander Edwards, Chief Garcia, Lt. Maelstrom and a complement of twenty armed U.S. Coast Guard law enforcement personnel take a skiff over.

Just as Jacob steps on the deck of the cruise ship, Bliss chimes in on his radio. "Sir, the crews of the barge and tanker have overwhelmed the pirates and are asking for help."

"What the…? This just keeps getting weirder and weirder. Send a skiff to each ship and assess the situation and provide help as needed. And Phillips…"

"Yes sir?"

"…You cover their asses with that OTO Melara. If anyone tries anything, you start blowing holes in the attacking ship."

Commander Edwards and his complement make it up to the top deck where the hostages are being held. Cheers, sighs of relief, and exasperated cries are all that can be heard. Jacob's radio chirps and Lt. Maelstrom, the security contingent commander, says, "We got them all sir. Well, they are saying one is unaccounted for. They did not even put up a fight. Frankly sir, they are scared out of their minds."

Jacob responds, "We need to find that last pirate. There are fifteen hundred civilians on this ship and about one hundred and fifty crew; God knows where he's hiding."

Phillips pipes in, "Sir, the cruise ship captain says that as far as he knows, he lost fourteen crew members, ten civilians, and five Mexican security specialists when they were boarded. The pirates demanded to know the location of all the VIP's that came on at Cozumel."

"And where would that be?" Jacob asks as lights start flashing in his head.

"They are pretty close to where you are, sir. The girls wanted the party at the highest point on the ship. The captain would not let them do it outside, so they are in the banquet hall just below you."

Instantly, Jacob, Roberto, and three others run down the stairs and into the hall. They see about two dozen Latina girls, all decked out in their party dresses, who look like they have been crying for hours. At least two look pretty beaten up. They hear a loud scream from the kitchen and the sound of slapping and cursing in Spanish.

One of the girls says in broken English, "It is Marnia, he take her last, say it is her birthday present. He already have me and two others today."

Jacob glares in the direction of the kitchen. Commander Edwards was known to have different fuses for different things, and the one for this disgusting act was not long at all. His vision turns red as his temples swell with blood that pours into his face. He heads for the source of the noise. Roberto and the rest lag behind to assess the scene and calm the girls.

Jacob rushes into the galley and kicks in the center office door. There, laying on the floor with her clothes torn off and her face a bloody mess is Marnia Gonzalez, the daughter of the president of Mexico. Standing over her is a stocky Jamaican man with long braided hair and a totally shocked look that turns to pure horror as he stares into Commander Jacob Edward's vehement and wrathful eyes. All Jacob can think as he slams his fists into the face and body of this rapist pirate is that the little girl this beast wants to maul looks very much like his own little Danielle.

The pirate is a formidable fighter but he does not have a chance. Jacob, a true master at hand-to-hand combat, uses all his artistic ability on this piece of shit. When he is done, he grabs the half-breathing bag of bruised meat and broken bones by his long-braided hair and drags him out into the hall and up the stairs to the top deck.

Roberto catches up to him and grabs him by the shoulder. He pleads with him to stop, but Jacob tells him and everyone else to stand down, "I am in command here." Jacob spies the small ladder that leads to the little observation platform in the front part of the top deck. With one hand on the rails and the other clutching the half conscious pirate's chocolate braided locks of greasy hair, he drags him up the ladder onto the little platform, picks him up to his shoulders and heaves him through the air into the dark Caribbean ocean some eight stories below. That is the last act that Commander Jacob Edwards will ever do as the captain of the *Hamilton-class* cutter, *First Responder*, United States Coast Guard.

Washington D.C. One Week Later

Commander Jacob Edwards sits in the office of the United States Coast Guard Commandant, along with his own commanding officer Captain Harrington, Vice Commandant Admiral Harrington, Will's father, and the Secretary of Homeland Security of the United States, discussing the Cozumel incident.

The commandant says, "Well now we all know how the barge and tanker got there. The pirates had people planted in their crews and when the cruise ship left

Cozumel, they mutinied and intercepted it. When the pirate clipper showed up with that big nonworking cannon on its deck, the cruise ship captain didn't know it was a fake and let that yacht dock with them. Then twenty-five people boarded the ship and stayed there for about eight hours until Commander Edwards' cutter showed up. He encountered the cutter first, tried to position himself between the pirate cutter and the cruise ship, and was then attacked by Goon Guns mounted on the deck at different locations. Two shots were fired at our cutter, at which point Commander Edwards returned fire with the OTO Melara and did significant damage to the stern of the pirate's cutter."

"That is correct, sir," says Captain Harrington.

"And then sniper fire was directed specifically at Commander Edwards from the fleeing cutter. Three shots I believe?"

"Correct again, sir," the captain responds.

The commandant looks at Jacob and says, "Up unto this point, all by the book, and very professionally done, Commander. But then you board the ship yourself, find a pirate raping the daughter of the Mexican president, beat the hell out of him, and drag him to the highest point you can find on that ship, and toss him off into the sea below."

Captain Harrington clears his throat and says, "That about sums it all up, sir."

The secretary looks at everyone and just sighs. "Jacob, you're a damn hero all over the Caribbean. The Mexican parliament has already awarded you with their highest military honor and has told our president if we prosecute you for killing that pirate, they are going to petition to extradite you and give you asylum. Gonzalez wants the president to grant you a full and complete pardon immediately. The piece of shit you executed at high seas killed three Mexican security officials, raped three girls, and killed one. That was not some ordinary pirate. He is wanted down there in half-a-dozen countries for rape, murder, piracy, human trafficking, child molestation, and in some circles is considered a pretty good assassin-for-hire. Hell, he was a champion MMA fighter in Jamaica for almost four years before he became a professional criminal. You went through him like he was a cripple."

"Well, in his defense," Jacob smirks, then continues, "I did catch him with his pants down, Mr. Secretary."

"You think this is funny, Edwards?" Admiral Harrington barks. "My Coast Guard is no place for a half-cocked cowboy like you, and especially commanding one of our best ships. I knew it was a mistake putting you in command. You were way overboard when you illegally threw that man overboard."

"Harrington, pipe down," says the commandant. "It just so happens I am in command of your Coast Guard, and I approved Edwards' Command of the *First Responder*. Let's not forget that in the grand scheme of things, the Coast Guard only fired one shot during the whole incident, managed to save over ninety-nine percent of the lives of everyone involved, and caught three out of the four ships."

"Well, yes, the Navy did overtake the pirate's cutter, but we took off half of its ass before it left. By the way, Captain, did we ever figure out where those backwoods pirates got the finances to put a brand new turbo diesel in that old cutter of theirs? Hell, it almost outran the naval battleship that chased it down."

"That is still under investigation, sir," the younger Captain Harrington replies.

Admiral Harrington says, "I am taking over the entire investigation of this matter personally, sir, don't worry, I'll get to the bottom of it very quickly."

The commandant glares at Harrington and says, "I am sure you will, Admiral. Now, for the matter of Edwards, uh, executing that murdering slimeball rapist. It's a problem, but I think we have come up with a workable solution. With your permission, Mr. Secretary?"

"Of course, Commandant, by all means. Go ahead."

The commandant continues. "Jacob, the president does not want this thing blowing up any more than it has." He eyeballs Admiral Harrington. "Almost everybody is on your side including me. We don't want to court martial you, Son, and no one anywhere is pressing charges. Hell, if you showed up in Mexico City today, they'd have a parade in your honor. But we can't, in all fairness, even appear to condone our ship commanders executing criminals at high seas. This isn't the nineteenth century. Son, if you will agree to retire, the secretary here has been authorized by the president to give you a full and honorable discharge with all the benefits befitting your nineteen years of service."

Jacobs' look of relief is abundantly apparent, but Admiral Harrington's deep scowl makes it clear he is irritated.

Jacob says, "Sir, I find that totally acceptable. Please let the president know that I am grateful for this act of mercy on my behalf."

Admiral Harrington, beet red, jumps out of his chair and says, "I don't find this acceptable at all! How can we even pretend to condone such behavior? Do you know this half-cocked cowboy hung up on me when I was trying to advise him during the situation?"

The Secretary of Homeland Security leans into Harrington, one inch away from his face and says, "Harrington, the whole conversation is a matter of taped record. He was under attack and you were putting him and his crew in danger with all your posturing antics. Now shut up and sit down."

The commandant stands up and dismisses everyone except the admiral. Jacob shakes the secretary's hand and walks out with Captain William Harrington into the hall.

"What's your dad got against me anyway, Will?" Jacob asks.

The captain just sighs, looks at his friend and says, "Dad thought I should take command of your ship when it came up but for some reason the commandant wanted you. You have been on dad's shitlist ever since."

"Why didn't you ever tell me, Will?"

"Oh, that would've made for a great commanding officer relationship between us, a real good morale booster, huh?"

"Yeah, I guess you're right Will, sorry."

"That's okay Jacob. What are you going to do now?"

Jacob smiles a little, looks at his friend and says, "You know I was never going past twenty years anyway. I was going to turn down that promotion and ship. I'm going home. My dad wants me to take over the business someday, and to tell you the truth I am really looking forward to it. I think Mary and Danielle are going to be ecstatic about the whole thing."

He smiles, shakes Will's hand, makes his final goodbyes, and then turns and leaves his friend in the hall as he walks away to his new life. Just then, Admiral Harrington steps out of the commandant's office and motions his son to a break room.

"Well, that did not go as planned at all," the elder Harrington says, "and our benefactor is very pissed off about the whole thing."

Will asks, "Is the whole deal off now, Dad?"

"No," the admiral says, "but he says it's going to take twice as long to set things up."

"Dad, it wasn't our fault that those crazy pirates decided to test out those Goon Guns."

"Yes, I know, Son. I am sure that the cannon on the deck of the pirate's cutter had Jacobs' complete attention until then."

Will sighs. "Too bad it messed up the way it did, but if he still thinks we can pull this off then Edwards' company will be nothing compared to Harrington Enterprises."

The admiral's brows furrow and with a grave look he says, "Never forget that Edwards Auto is a big key to this all working and we just suffered a major setback with glamour boy going home to start running the place. But our friend is the very best at what he does and I am sure he's got some elaborate contingency plan."

"Yes, Dad. I'm sure he does."

CHAPTER TWO
IT RUNS IN THE FAMILY

Present Day

She needs to run. It's her time and no one else belongs. A little more stretching and she can hit the road. Sometimes it is three miles, sometimes eight. It does not matter only as long as she gets her fix. She doesn't know why she puts it like that; it's not like she ever took drugs or had a drinking problem. It's just that running always gets rid of the pain, at least for a while. It's funny how much her stamina and speed has increased over the last few months. She laughs, remembering her eight-mile run at a 7:45 clip per mile two weeks ago.

When she told someone at the studio, they thought she should start doing 5k and 10k runs, maybe even a marathon or something. But that would defeat the whole purpose of the thing. The last thing she wants is to turn this into a competition that she could win or lose. It's the reason she moved down here in the first place, to get away. Think. Grieve. Find out what and who Danielle is and who she is going to be. It broke Grandpa's heart when he found out she was leaving, poor old guy. She's all he has left, and she knows it. He wanted her to have everything, run everything; be the boss. That job was supposed to be Daddy's. He was the smart one; the great pirate-fighting Coast Guard commander of South Texas. Responsibility to him was just fun; the more, the better.

Mom loved Daddy, and she loved her little Danielle too. She had said, "You're just two people with the same brain—all brawn and all go. You both have enough steam to fly to the moon and back and still stay up half the night planning something for the next day."

Grandma had said, "Let's all go to Australia together. It will be wonderful, just the five of us together taking some time to relax and enjoy each other. Grandma was such a kind soul, so tender and gentle. Danielle would never have fathomed that her dad could come from such a gentle woman without knowing Grandpa. Grandpa said "no" to Australia of course—too busy, too much going on at headquarters or "HQ" as he liked to call it. Not a good time to get away. Danielle also said "no"; she had a recital and finals for her senior year coming up and everyone agreed she shouldn't go.

But to everyone's surprise, Daddy said "yes". So off they went, Mom, Dad, and Grandma, flying out of Baltimore-Washington International. Grandpa dropped them off and Danielle said goodbye on Facetime.

The next few days are all just a blur to her. All she remembers is Grandpa calling her on the phone, crying and screaming uncontrollably, "I never should've let them go. It's my fault; I knew it was the wrong time of year to go down there."

Eventually, Grandpa's shop foreman frontline man, Tony, got on the phone, "Danielle, I'm sorry, it's about your mom, dad and grandmother. Their plane went missing about an hour ago and no one knows anything."

Danielle remembers rushing to the computer and calling up the flight, then searching every news outlet. No one knew anything; authorities had lost all contact with the plane. The U.S. Navy was scouring the area, but no one had any answers.

She panicked, got in her car and drove like a madwoman, all the way back to Manheim from school in Philadelphia. The Schuylkill wasn't that bad yet, which was good because she was a maniac pushing that little Jetta for everything it had. When she got to HQ, Tony said, "He's in his office."

Grandpa was face down on his desk. The office was in shambles. There were papers everywhere and a broken water glass on the floor next to the door. He was still crying, shaking wildly, his eyes bloodshot. No one had ever feared for his health before, he was the toughest old bird she had ever known. He could keep up with most men half his age, except his son of course. But Danielle was scared he might have a heart attack. She did the only thing she could. She ran up to him and fell into his arms and starting shaking and crying with him.

The news came the next day. Their connecting plane, Flight 1247 from Los Angeles to Australia, crash landed in the Pacific Ocean. An explosion on board was deemed the cause, investigation pending. No survivors presumed.

Now more than three years since that terrible day, she remembers just being a robot going from one thing to another—first the funeral, then the dance recital, finals, and graduation. She graduated college, magna cum laude, at Temple University. She did everything that everyone expected out of her, what she expected out of herself, but it was empty.

She tried hard that summer to help Grandpa. Summer was Manheim's busy season, with so many cars. It was the biggest auto auction in the whole world and her grandfather was one of the crown princes of the sale, averaging from 800 to 1200 units a week. Jim's shop did it all—detailing, auto painting, paintless dent removal, mechanical, and upholstery. He bought wholesale units from all over the country and even the world, bringing them to Manheim, shaping them up and selling them at the auction. He had almost a hundred employees now and was ranked with the top five wholesalers in the world.

Danielle knew the business from the ground up. She could easily go in and take anyone's place and do a superb job whether in the shop or the office. She was the best, next to her dad anyway. Grandpa did too, but that did not count. He built that business from the ground up and all that stuff was just in his blood. Everywhere she turned, she saw her mother bringing something to the shop, her dad grabbing her to go have lunch somewhere where they could just talk. She saw Grandma doing her best to make Grandpa spend some quality time with her, which he always did, if not a little begrudgingly at first. They were all so happy. Then it just vanished in a flash.

She had originally planned on further education, but that fall, just before grad school was to start, she told Grandpa she was not going. He hit the ceiling, not because she was not going back to school—he always thought that was a waste of time anyway—but because she said she was taking some time off and going back to South Texas to do volunteer work for a while and teach dance to underprivileged girls.

"Why the hell do you want to do that? You're needed here, I need you here! This place is meaningless without you!"

She did love HQ. The whole thing ran in her blood too. Few people could hold a candle to Danielle when it came to the automotive wholesale biz, but it just hurt too much. It was a family business, and the family was devastated, torn apart by an inexplicable and undeserved tragedy.

Oh, he was mad all right, but the last thing he said to her as she slammed the door and walked out was "I love you; I will always be here for you. It's all yours whenever you want it."

Her heart races, sweat streams out of every pore in her body. She wheezes and coughs, finishing her run. Tears stream down her face. Sobbing and bleary eyed, she looks at her stopwatch. Sixty minutes flat. She just passed the eight-mile mark. That's eight miles at a 7:30 clip, a record for her, but it's the only way she can deal with the memories, by running. The harder she runs, the more she can think about it and work it out, the more she can deal with the pain.

She tried cardio boxing, but that just reminded her of her dad and the countless hours in the dojo, back yard, boxing gym, and judo rooms practicing every type of fighting known to man. She couldn't dance it out because mom and grandma loved to go to every recital she ever did since she was four years old. Running was different. Sure, she did it before, but only in training and never in competition, and she was going to keep it that way. She regained control of herself, walked back to her apartment, and got into the shower to get ready to go teach her girls—like she'd been doing almost every day for over three years now.

Danielle Edwards was not a small girl, but you could not call her large either; one hundred and forty pounds of muscle and sinew, an avid athlete her whole life. She started martial arts training at six years old and dance at four—limber and wily as a cat. In junior high and high school, she competed in soccer and swimming. Jacob personally taught her boxing and judo, and some other martial arts. She had an uncanny head for business and especially sales, and she knew cars like few others. She had always loved working in Grandpa's shop, and wasn't afraid to get her hands dirty whether it was detailing, auto body or auto mechanics and upholstery. She knew it all and could do it all. Everybody always said with Jacob and Danielle around, Jim could just sit back and take it easy, take Linda on a long second honeymoon and not worry about a thing. Fat chance of that. Jim Edwards loved fun as much as the next guy, but HQ was in his blood and he couldn't leave it.

As Danielle stepped out of the shower, her cell rang. It was Grandpa. Thursday before sale, he probably wanted help on registrations. That was his least favorite thing about the business and Danielle and her dad were always much better at it than he was.

"No, Grandpa you can't put all those nice low-mile Japanese units in lane nineteen, that's the dealer consignment and everything is sold there. You want to target your market on the block and on line. Yes, I know it's more expensive, but if we get them all in the same block and with buyers who are looking for them, you'll sell more and for a better price."

A buzz came over the intercom. Barbara in the front office says, "Boris is out front and wants to talk to you, Jim. What should I tell him?"

"Tell him I will be right out."

The annoying huff comes over the phone. "What does he want now?" Danielle asks. "Is he keeping up on rent and utilities, Grandpa?"

Jim chuckles a little and says, "Boris has his faults but he's been a good tenant so far, and a very profitable client.

Until I get my diesel mechanic shop fully functional, I have nothing to put in that whole new building you and your dad talked me into adding." Jim's cheeks flush a little. "Sorry honey, didn't mean to bring up the hurt."

"That's okay, Grandpa, we have to learn to talk about them without breaking down. Keep an eye on Boris. There is more going on with him than we know. Oh, and would you tell Yuri to stop hitting on me every time he's down here. He gives me the creeps and Grandpa Roberto is about to shoot him."

Jim thanks Danielle and hangs up. He knows she's right, but it feels like the auction is squeezing him again. God knows those big lease companies don't pay out the nose for these lanes, but Jim knows that is just the nature of the beast. Man, he sure misses that little girl. She's smart as a whip and just as pretty as her grandma was when they got married all those years ago. Danielle is the only person he had ever paid that compliment to, and he meant it with all his heart.

Jim goes out to the front lot and there stands a tall, dark-headed, distinguished looking man in front of some pimped-out 2013 Hummer. Jim sticks his thumbs in the front part of his belt, laughs, and says, "Boris, for once you and I agree because there is no way in hell I would get a condition report on that ghetto mobile."

"Oh Jim, I will get all the money for this tomorrow and no online condition report is going to help me do better." This was an old argument. Boris had been a client for about eight years. He and his nephew Yuri were good wholesalers with sources all over the country, even as far west as California and Washington, and yes, even South Texas. Boris did not get condition reports or CRs for any of his units. He did over one hundred units a week lately, which made him one of Jim's more profitable clients. Boris ran only on lane nineteen no matter what he had and most of his sales were online to overseas clients. What was really surprising, however, was how fast the units were paid for and shipped. None of this ever stopped Jim from egging him on about CRs and PDR, paintless dent removal.

"Boris, you know you have about ten units back there that could use PDR. My guy Alan could do them all for a buck fifty apiece."

Boris gives his usual comeback, "Jim, Jim, what do people in South America and Asia care about dents? They just want a motor that works and something with air conditioning."

"Okay, okay," Jim says in a conciliatory manner, then adds, "Hey, when you want to make changes in my building, please clear it with me first! Boarding off those windows like that will turn that shop into a sweat box."

"Yes, but I'll save tons of money on my heating bill this winter, won't I Jim?"

"Maybe, but if I have to repair those frames someday, you're paying for it not me."

"Okay Jim, as usual you drive a hard bargain. So, have you thought about my offer? It is generous and you could retire in ease. It must be so hard for you here all by yourself with no family. You could move down to South Texas and be with Danielle and Mary's family."

With a hint of jovial sarcasm Jim replies, "Boris your concern for me is quite touching but if I move down there, I still can't get away from all this. Yuri shows up about twice a month anyway and never misses an opportunity to call Danielle."

"Yes, yes, my nephew is quite taken with your granddaughter, maybe a partnership through marriage is what we should be discussing, hey?"

Jim lets out an emphatic geez and says, "This isn't 1901 in Russia, Boris. I think Danielle would probably kick both our heads off at the stump if she even thought I would entertain such a concept. Besides, she doesn't want the business anymore."

Boris slyly smiles as he smokes his Cuban cigar. "All the more reason to sell to me my friend."

Jim puts a hand on each hip and says, "Boris, did I ever tell you about my mentor and friend J.R. down in Alabama? He was the biggest new car dealer in the whole state; had an empire that dwarfs my little operation. He ran every aspect of it for almost seventy years. He would probably still be at it but he died falling off a horse at ninety-two years old. Don't suspect that I am any different than him. Well, I have to go. Have all your units done and ready to go by five, okay buddy?"

Boris half nods a less than enthusiastic gesture as Jim walks away, and then mumbles under his breath, "Horses come in many forms, my old friend."

Boris gets back in his pimped-out Hummer and drives behind the north building on the property, gets out his iPhone, and calls Yuri whom he sent down to South Texas a week ago, supposedly to buy some more cars for next month's sales.

"Yes, Uncle, what do you want?"

"Have you made any progress this time?"

"I am telling you, she does not like me, I am not her type. She practically loathes me and yet you expect me to somehow woo this stuck-up debutante bitch to fall in love with and marry me?"

"No, you incredible idiot, all we need is to make sure that she gets on our yacht with her grandfather next month. Everything else is taken care of."

"But how?" Yuri asks.

"Well if your boyish charm is insufficient, we must find another sentimentality to use to bend her to our plan."

Yuri sarcastically adds, "The only thing she cares about is her mother's family, and those children she teaches dance."

Boris is agitated with his stupid nephew's lack at seeing the obvious. "No! You stay as far away from Roberto and that group as you can. We don't need to get the Coast Guard's attention again, nor do I want the FBI sniffing around. You have got to play this just right or we will be the ones experiencing a catastrophic explosion in more ways than one. I have some friends in the Russian Ballet Academy; perhaps there is an angle we could work if we are patient and wise."

"What could that little dancer boy Alyeks do for us?" Yuri asks, immediately sorry he said it.

Boris closes the connection and navigates to Alyeks Yeshlton's phone number on his contact list.

Alyeks answers. "Boris, my friend what could you possibly want this early in the morning?"

"Alyeks, I am thinking that you need to come to the United States to do some talent scouting say in South Texas next month?"

Alyeks is completely taken back as he says, "Boris, Boris, I admit that I owe you a great debt for all you and your associates did to get me the senior dance instructor position here, but what possible reason would I have to recruit dancers from Texas, of all places? Do they even know what ballet is in that land of cowboys and Indians?"

"For starters, Alyeks, it should not concern you why I want you here, only that I do and therefore you will come. I will make the arrangements with your superiors and send you all you need to make the trip."

"Okay, Boris, but please just tell me what we are really doing."

"Well for one, we are going to see Danielle Edwards with her grandfather. She has been instructing at a not-for-profit ballet school in South Texas for over three years, and I hear she has some rather passionate dancers who would be overwhelmed to dance for the great Alyeks Yeshlton of the renowned Russian Ballet Academy of Moscow."

"Well, Boris, I admit that at one time Danielle Edwards did show incredible ability for an American, but she is way past her prime now, and does not have the experience to teach here."

Boris gives a sly chuckle and says, "Alyeks you are one the world's true artists but sometimes I think you are as dull as my nephew Yuri. You are going down to act like you are interested in looking at the students of the studio. I want Danielle to believe one of her students has a real chance. Do you think you can handle that with an appearance of competence?"

"Of course, Boris, of course." Alyeks hangs up the phone and draws a deep breath. He knows he has no choice; Boris owns him. He does whatever Boris tells him to do, no matter how much he despises the man and his business. *You have to die someday you vicious old bastard,* he thinks to himself, *then I will be free of my obligations to you and do only what I love; dance.*

His sheets are a mess, and in the early morning soft blue glow of the bedroom all he can see are two very muscular thighs wrapped around a pillow protruding from the sheets. "Who was that Alyeks, why so early?"

"Nothing to be concerned about my young precious girl, go back to sleep. You have a lot of work for tomorrow, that second act will be very difficult for you."

"Mmm, it could not be any more than what you put me through last night, lover."

Alyeks lies down and places his hand on a very firm and well-trained bottom and drifts back to a fitful and exhausting sleep.

Boris knows Alyeks will do whatever he tells him to do. *Damn,* he thinks, *I hope he does not try anything with some young girls down there.* Those South Texas peasants will not accept that sort of thing. Boris will allow nothing to interfere with his plans for Jim and Danielle Edwards.

34

CHAPTER THREE
ALL IN A DAY'S WORK

Edwards Auto

Alan yells, "What the hell are you doing? This is Jim's car and he wants it done tonight!"

"No," Ivan says. "No PDR, Boris' orders."

"I don't care what that old shriveled up Russian says." Alan points his finger in Ivan's face. "This isn't his car and I have a work order to prove it."

Boris walks up to a rather heated argument behind his detail shop. "What is going on over here? An old shriveled up Russian would like to know."

Ivan runs up to Boris and speaks in Russian frantically like he is pleading for his life. Boris' eyes bore into Ivan's like he wants his younger employee to just melt in front of him. Then with the practiced patience of a domineering and less than trustworthy politician, Boris turns his attention to Jim Edward's best PDR man, Alan.

"Well, Alan, let me see that work order of yours and I will get to the bottom of your misunderstanding."

"There's no misunderstanding here. That's Jim's 2013 Camry and he wants me to do PDR on it tonight."

Ivan turns red with desperation and anger while he shouts, "No, he can't stick rods in those panels, he might tear lose all that mo—"

Boris grabs his collar. "Shut up you imbecile, go back to the shop and work on the other vehicles, I will deal with you later."

Boris pulls out his smartphone and calls up his auction app. He looks at it for a second then says, "Now I see from my online account that this is indeed Jim's vehicle, but what you do not know is that Jim just sold it to me today and I am putting it in my own inventory. The changes have not made it to the Edwards' files yet."

"Oh great," Alan says, "now I'm out another hundred and fifty bucks for a go around."

"Don't worry my friend, I'll make it up to you. Here, have dinner on me." Boris reaches into his pocket, pulls out a one hundred dollar bill and gives it to Alan.

"Works for me," says Alan, as he shoves it into his pocket. He grabs his tools and moves on to the next car.

He mumbles to himself that he wishes they were all that easy, but those Russians sure give him the creeps.

Boris picks up his phone and calls a very familiar number in his contacts. "Jim, this is Boris, I have a request. You have a pearl red 2013 Toyota Camry back here; the last eight of the VIN are D0063487. I would like to purchase it from you."

Jim's smile is huge because he knows when a dealer calls him on a vehicle the night before the sale, the guy already has it sold and wants it pretty bad. "Sure, twenty-three five will buy it."

"Jim that is absurd. The Manheim Market Report on it is only just over twenty-two thousand."

"Yes," says Jim, "but you know it could go as high as twenty-four five in the right lane at the right time."

"Jim, you spend too much money on those overpriced lanes. You've been talking to Danielle again, have you not?"

"Well, she's always steered me in the right direction on sale day just like her daddy did. Twenty-three thousand five hundred is my last offer or it is selling on that overpriced lane tomorrow."

"Okay, I will buy it. Please see that it is transferred to my account immediately."

"No problem, Boris, nice doing business with you."

As he turns to walk back to his rented and very private shop, he thinks, *now I have two things to hold Ivan accountable for—losing over a thousand on that deal is definitely the lesser of the two.*

Back in South Texas

After a one-hour record run and two hours of dance rehearsal, Danielle is beat. Of course, if Juan would have shown up for class, she never would have had to take his place in rehearsal. Sometimes that boy drives her out of her mind. He is such a fantastic, raw talent, a true expert in Latino salsa dancing. He showed up at the studio two years ago and said he wanted to learn ballet, or at least his mother wanted him to. It did not take Danielle long to see that the boy was definitely something special. He had a rare gift that if properly cultivated could really open some major doors for him. She knew the problem; a sixteen-year-old Spanish boy doing ballet is not the most macho thing for a guy in his peer group. He was sure to be down at the boy's boxing gym again.

Danielle got into her 1972 Buick Skylark that Grandpa Roberto let her drive while she lived down here. Boy, if Daddy could see her now, he would be so jealous. Roberto never let anyone touch that completely restored and reconditioned classic. It was Chevy green with a thick white racing stripe coming down the backside of the roof through the sail panels and into the front door, a half-white vinyl top, and racing mags on the back with the old Goodyear symbol on them. It is every bit a teenager's dream car, and she knows it is going to have good impact where she is headed.

She pulls up around back at the local Boys Club Community Center where the boxers train. She exits the car to a cacophony of whistles and cat calls. Juan sees her pull up and immediately tries to make himself incognito.

She just doesn't get it. This is no place for her to show up and give him a hard time, especially in front of all his homies. He knows that only a few of the cat calls were directed at the Buick; the rest were for her, his dance instructor, the girl on the verge of majorly embarrassing him yet again.

Danielle flashes her sale-day smile, the one that left most of the old farts at the auto auction speechless, as she walks up to all the teens who are paying her no small amount of attention. Juan is over by the heavy bag. He is holding it for a very muscular Latino boy who probably weighs about one-eighty and can definitely put some strength into his body work punches. Juan is also a very muscular boy of about one hundred and fifty pounds. He has some skills of his own in the boxing category, but is definitely an admirer of his powerful friend's ability.

Danielle looks at Juan with deep concern and says, "Why did you miss practice? The girls were very disappointed today."

"I know, I'll see you *mañana*, okay *Maestra* Danielle?"

"No, Juan, I need to talk to you today. I had to do all your parts today, and frankly I am a little upset." Snickers and chuckles erupt all around Juan as his buddies start to tease him about his dancing.

"Juan," says the big kid punching the heavy bag, "Why do you hang with all these girls so much? A little *chica* like this can do your job, so why do you come here? You want us to teach you how to be a man?"

With a pensive but frustrated voice, Juan says, "Shut up, Ricky."

"Why don't you make me shut up, little sissy salsa boy?"

Danielle sees the situation is getting out of hand, so she sets her eyes over on Ricky and says, "Hey lightweight. You don't look so tough. I bet you couldn't handle holding that bag for a little girl like me."

"What are you kidding, baby doll? Bring it on! My dad is a heavyweight contender and I hold the bag for him all the time, you'll just hurt yourself pounding on our bag."

"Okay, showboat, hold it then."

"Sure *chica*, but if you don't budge me, I get a kiss okay?"

Danielle grins from ear to ear; he just went for the bait. "You are on, Don Juan, and if I do budge you, then you will be responsible to see that no one ever bugs Juan again about his dancing, deal?"

"Sure, baby. It's your funeral."

Danielle steps up to the super hundred and twenty pound bag that Ricky is holding, checks out his stance and looks for his weakest balance angle. She positions her body in the proper middle fighting stance for the move she has planned. She knows she only weighs one hundred and forty pounds and the bag and the boy are almost three hundred combined, but she's got his balance pegged. These guys are all strength punchers and don't seem to understand how to throw a power strike like her dad taught her. Even so, if she threw her best punch, she probably would barely budge him, and she wants to make a damn good impression on all these teen boys that usually think with the wrong head anyway.

No one said she had to punch the bag with her fists. She faces the bag with her right hand forward, and someone laughs, "Southpaw!" She ignores it as she twists her head first to the left and then jumps straight up bringing her left knee as high as she can into her chest. She whips her head and shoulders around full circle to face the bag and sling shots a perfect jumping side kick into the top quarter part of the bag. The impact is immediate. Ricky loses his light grip on both sides of the bag as it slams into his face and chest, propelling him almost eight feet into the cinder block wall behind him. The impact knocks the wind out of him and he falls face first to the ground. Danielle lands in a perfect left lead stance as the whole yard erupts in clapping, whoops, and hollers.

As she and Juan walk over to help Ricky off the floor, Danielle says to herself, "I think Daddy would've been proud of the way I calculated that one." Ricky looks at Danielle with a kind of fearful respect, and the beginning of a crush that will haunt him for the rest of his life.

"You remember the deal, Ricky, no one gives Juan a hard time about dancing, okay?" Danielle orders. "Oh, and by the way, I could barely fill in for Juan today because he is a much more powerful dancer than I am. And if I did not dance there is no way I could kick like that."

Ricky, fully owned, answers, "Yes, *Maestra*, no one will ever say anything to Juan again about dancing while I am around, *comprende amigos?*"

All respond with a resounding, "*Sí!*"

Danielle smiles at Juan. "Can I give you a lift? You can drive, but if you tell my grandpa, I'll kill you."

"Sure!" says Juan as he runs ahead of Danielle to get in the driver's seat. Juan is on his phone when Danielle pulls out the keys from her purse and gets into the passenger seat. She buckles up, and tells Juan to buckle up too as she hands him the keys.

Juan lives about a half mile out of town in a small farm house his family has owned for generations. When they pull up to the front of the house, Danielle's eyes about pop out of their sockets. In front of Juan's house, outside the barn, his father stands next to a 1967 Ford Mustang Fastback. Although it looks like it has seen better days, she immediately notices that the chrome bumpers are in fairly good condition. Although in need of a paint job, the body looks pretty sound as well. All of Danielle's exhaustion is immediately forgotten as she jumps out of the Skylark and practically flies over to the piece of pure automotive poetry in front of her.

"Hello Danielle. Juan told me you were bringing him home from the gym and I thought you would like to see this. It was my father's, and I am thinking of selling it," Juan's father says with a devious smile. "I have not had it running much for the last fifteen years. It's just been sitting in the barn. I did have it covered up in this tarp so it is not really bad. I was hoping you could tell me how much it is worth. Juan never wants to help me work on it and I just don't have the time to do it myself."

"Papa, you know we always get into a fight when we try to work on this thing and neither of us knows what we are doing."

Juan's dad sighs and says,"Yes, I know. I'm just a truck driver and not very knowledgeable about car restoration, but we can use online videos and figure it out together."

"Online videos? *Aye yi yi*, Papa, that is so stupid we need to send this to an expert to do it right. This is a classic car and deserves the best."

Danielle's mind goes three thousand miles-a-second as she devours every inch of the automotive excellence sitting in front of her. "You're right Juan, this car does deserve the best, but we can give it to her if we all work together."

"What do you mean 'we'?"

"I mean we, the three of us can restore this little beauty to factory mint perfection, and Mr. Torres, if you still want to sell it when we are done, my grandfather could find you about a half dozen guys that will pay you enough money to cover more than half of Juan's college expenses."

Juan and his dad just stare at Danielle in a mixture of hope, excitement, and profound doubt. "Are you sure Danielle?" they both say.

"Are you kidding?" Danielle exclaims, "this is like *Christmas in Wonderland* for me. Let me see, I have about three hours before I have to go to Grandpa Roberto's grand opening to wait tables. I can give you about two and a half hours if you let me clean up here."

"Sure!" both Torres' say simultaneously. "Okay, let's get started. And Juan, if I do this with you, then you have to promise never to miss another rehearsal like today, okay?"

Juan looks devastated that Danielle just said that in front of his father but replies, "Yes, *Maestra*, I promise no more missing."

Miguel takes his hat off and swats his sixteen-year-old son across the back of the head with it. "Are you *loco hombre*?! Your mother will skin us both alive if you screw up this studio opportunity."

"I'm sorry, Papa, but you should've seen what Danielle did at the boxing gym today. She almost knocked Ricky out when he held the bag for her and—"

"Juan!" Danielle interjects, "let's get started."

"*Si, Maestra*."

After a quick trip to the automotive parts store for some basic detailing and auto body supplies, the three of them get right at it. Two hours later, Juan and Danielle are working on the rear bumper with an electric drill and a small buffing pad attached to it.

"Juan, hold the pad directly to the bumper and put the RPM's at about half. Polish a five-inch section at a time, and don't move on until all the blemishes are gone. If the polish gets a little gummy, just add more, or use the Snappy Shine to lubricate it a little. Don't worry about the mess on the car; we will clean that up later. That's it. Miguel, just use the cheese grater tool and slide it over the hard putty at an angle in both directions, then do it the opposite way. Yup, you want it to follow the contours of the body style so when you sand and prime, it looks natural."

"Okay guys, I've got to get to Grandpa Roberto's grand opening, so I am going in to clean up."

Miguel smiles, "Just see Angela, she will help you."

"Thanks Miguel." Danielle quickly cleans up and gets ready for work. Boy was that fun. She remembers helping her dad and grandpa Roberto restore the Skylark. While she drives away from Juan's house, she thinks to herself how anyone can think of that as work? Restoring autos was never a day's work to her, it was just as fun as dancing.

*   *   *

Tonight is the grand opening of Grandpa Roberto's new bar and grill. It's funny that he's so concerned about keeping the name of the new place a secret. The sign arrived only yesterday and he kept it under a canvas cover outside as they mounted it. He would not let anyone see the new menus, or any paraphernalia until the opening ceremony.

Danielle had worked at his little deli coffee bar in the gas station convenience store since she got here and helped Nana Isabella with the books as well. But Grandpa Roberto said it was her right to be a major part of the grand opening tonight, and one thing Danielle knew about her mother's dad was that he knew how to throw a party, so she was pretty excited about the whole thing by the time she got there.

As Danielle pulls up, she sees Grandpa Roberto out front with a couple of movers unloading yet another large piece of something into the main dining room. Roberto looks over at Danielle, and then at his Skylark, and gasps, "Danielle Isabella Edwards! What is all that red powder on my car?"

Oh, boy, thinks Danielle. She forgot to hose off the sanding dust from the Mustang that got on the Skylark at Miguel and Juan's place. "Sorry, Grandpa Roberto. I was over at Juan's and his dad showed me that 1967 Ford Mustang Fastback he has stored in his barn—which you never told me about by the way—and we started restoring it."

"Oh my God," says Roberto. "Now you will never get any sleep. There is a very good reason I did not tell you about that hot rod of Miguel's."

Danielle raises her hands, palms up, and exclaims, "But when that thing is done, it could practically put Juan through college, so I think it is a great idea."

Roberto gives his granddaughter a hello kiss and says, "I thought you said he's good enough to get a very nice dancing scholarship like you did."

"Yes, true, but college always has hidden expenses, you know."

"Oh, of that I am keenly aware, believe me; okay, so you have but another project to work on. Aye, Danielle, you wear me out like your father did."

"Thanks for the compliment Grandpa, what are we doing now?"

"We are about to get started. Just go see your nana and get your new uniform."

Danielle goes into the dining room and joins the crowd standing around Nana Isabella, which includes all the cooks, wait staff, hosts and hostesses, bartenders, and dishwashers.

Nana says, "We are expecting a very full house for the grand opening, so we are very grateful that everybody showed up." She starts handing out uniforms and shirts to everyone. All that they have on them is a capital *J* and a capital *L* on the right breast of the clothing. Danielle notices that the *L* looks a little funny with an extra line vertically and little horizontal lines in between. She asks her nana what is up with that and Isabella just says, "You will find out later, just put this on." Instead of a uniform, she hands Danielle a dress inside a dry cleaner package.

"What is this, Nana? Isn't this one of Mom's old dresses?"

"Well, yes, it is but I would not call it an old dress; it was very special to Mary, and now I want you to have it and wear it tonight."

"Okay, Nana, but is this really appropriate to be serving tables in?"

"Oh. Danielle, you are not serving tables tonight. Just stick with me, and Roberto will explain everything later."

Danielle donned her mother's very sexy and tight evening gown which was absolutely gorgeous, if not a little revealing. But she knew the Latina girls frequently dressed like this so she really did not feel out of place.

Danielle stuck with her nana for the next hour as the very excited mother of her mother whisked around the whole complex getting everything ready.

Time flies right into opening time and Grandpa Roberto gets everyone set inside; then he ushers in about forty Coast Guard officers and enlisted men who came from Brazos and Corpus Christi. In that group is someone who Danielle immediately recognizes. She runs up and gives a big hug to the man she affectionately calls Uncle Larry. Captain Larry Phillips, Sector Commander Corpus Christi, returns Danielle's hug with equal enthusiasm. "Oh my God, Uncle Larry, I didn't know you were coming!"

Larry puts on his sly smile and says, "Roberto and Isabella haven't told you what's up yet, have they?"

"No, and I feel like I am the only one here that doesn't know."

Just then a very handsome lieutenant approaches the pair and says, "Captain, we are about to start, sir."

"Thank you, Lieutenant. Danielle, may I introduce Lieutenant Chris Rottanelli. He has been recently stationed in this sector and will be in command of our new security patrol at station Brazos."

"It is a pleasure, Miss Edwards. Might I say you look breathtakingly lovely in that dress? This must be a very important occasion for you."

Larry pipes in before Rottanelli lets the cat out of the bag, "Uh, Lieutenant, I think you need to go and get ready to present the colors."

"Aye aye Captain, Miss Edwards." Rottanelli salutes his captain, grabs and kisses Danielle's hand, and walks off.

"Wow, that was refreshing," says Danielle as she steadies her racing heart.

"What do you mean, Danielle?" Larry asks.

"Well, usually these days when I meet a Coast Guard officer, or any military officer for that matter, and they hear my name, they want to fawn all over me about Daddy. But he just told me I am beautiful and complimented my mother's dress, and that was really nice. Is there someone who doesn't know who my dad was in the Coast Guard?"

Philips just laughs and jovially looks at Danielle, and replies "Do you really even think that is possible in this day and time, Danielle?"

"No, probably not, but that was really nice for a change. Is anyone going to tell me what is going on around here?"

Grandfather's voice comes over the loudspeaker, which is also being projected outside, from the center of the room where he stands at a microphone. "Danielle, could you please join Isabella and me up front. Captain Phillips, we would be honored if you come as well."

Larry offers his arm to Danielle and they both walk to the small stage in the center of the dining room where Roberto, Isabella, and her three uncles are waiting for them. Just as she steps on the stage, her heart goes into her throat when out of the corner of her eye she sees

Grandpa Edwards step onto the stage next to Danielle and Roberto.

Danielle is perplexed, ready to burst with confusion as she turns to Jim and says, "Grandpa, what are you doing here? I just talked to you like nine hours ago and you were in Manheim, getting ready for the sale."

Jim chuckles and says, "Yes honey, but Captain Phillips had a military transport pick me up at Lancaster Airport about two hours after we talked, and jetted me down here for this occasion."

Danielle rolls her eyes and gives a confused if exasperated gasp and says, "You mean to tell me that the military flew you down here for the grand opening of Grandpa Roberto's new bar and grill? Come on, what the hell is—"

"Excuse me, ladies and gentleman, but it is finally time," Roberto's amplified voice bellows to the audience. He looks nervously at Danielle. "First, I want to thank the United States Coast Guard and Corpus Christi Sector Commander, Captain Larry Phillips, for helping put this whole ceremony together. Over thirteen years ago, Captain Phillips and I got to serve on a mission under the command of one of the Coast Guard's most dynamic and passionate commanders, my son-in-law the late Commander Jacob Edwards." A resounding applause erupts both inside the dining room and outside in the parking lot with quite a few hoots and hollers as well. "Now, we all know that Jacob did not like pirates," —many chuckle heartily—"and we all know that the Cozumel incident is something they will not soon forget amongst the criminal elements of South Mexico and Central America. Although the Mexican government has fully acknowledged the heroism of Jacob and his crew, our own, up to this point, have not. But with the help of Captain Phillips, Jacob's second-in-command, and help of the vice president of the United States, who was the Commandant of the Coast Guard at the time, this restaurant has been granted the status of a National Historic Landmark. So without any further ado I present to you—my family, friends, neighbors, and shipmates— the dedication of *Jacob's Ladder*."

At that precise moment the sheets fall from the sign outside and the object inside. When Danielle sees what is under the sheet, she loses her breath and buries her head deep in Jim Edward's chest and begins to cry.

There, in the middle of the dining room, is the ladder and view plank from which Jacob threw the notorious, repulsive pirate after having dragged him by the locks of his braided hair all those years ago. As that sinks in, another sheet drops on the far wall to the left, and a life size aerial photo of the actual event covers the whole wall.

Roberto says, "Many of you probably have seen this Pulitzer Prize winning photograph taken by one of the news crews that flew down to Cozumel in long range helicopters that night."

Jim bends down and whispers in Danielle's ear, "You know I have been trying to buy that ladder for years from the cruise ship line but they would not let go of it because it was such a draw for customers. But after the vice president got the national landmark status through for Roberto's restaurant, they sent it right down. Hell, there is even talk about expanding the port here so the cruise ships can stop by to let people come and see it. Boy, if that ever happens, Roberto's going to be richer than we, uh, I mean *I* am."

"Oh stop it, you old kook!" Danielle sobs, wiping tears from her eyes. "I never said I'm giving everything up. I told you I just needed time."

"You have all the time you will ever need from me, honey. I just love you and want the best for you; you know that."

Roberto yells out, "The first round is on the house. The kitchen is open so eat up. Wait staff, let's go! Oh, and any of you enlisted coasties get out of line, you're going to answer to me personally!"

There is a jovial but nervous laugh from certain members in the crowd as everyone disperses to different areas of the restaurant.

Isabella comes up and hugs her granddaughter. "I am sorry, Danielle, but Roberto wanted it all to be a surprise and especially for you."

"Oh my God, Nana, I don't know what to say. This is so overwhelming, but Daddy deserves this and I can't thank you enough, all of you."

Isabella looks Danielle in the eyes with pure love and says, "Darling, I wanted to do something special for you tonight so I took out the dress your mother wore to the ball the night your father proposed to her, and fitted it to you and got it cleaned and ready for tonight. That is what you are wearing right now."

Danielle falls into her grandmother's arms and starts crying all over again.

After Danielle pulls herself together, she walks out to the parking lot to look at the sign. *Jacob's Ladder* is in big black letters, and the letter *L* looks like a ladder. She finally gets the new uniforms the staff is wearing.

"Hey, beautiful, you sure look fine in that dress, deserving of all my attention."

Danielle thinks, *Oh my God, not now.* This is kind of a recurring theme down here, the prettier the girl the more some of the boys think they own them. She's had to set a few straight over the last few years and has gotten quite good at it. But there was something familiar about this one's voice as she turns around to see Yuri, Boris' nephew. "Yuri, do you ever get tired of being a child in a man's body?"

Yuri has obviously been drinking as evidenced by his slurred response. "Well, I think that you would like to have this man's body, would you not?"

"I would not," Danielle shouts as she pushes Yuri out of her way.

"No woman treats me like that, you stuck-up bitch."

"Wow, Yuri, why don't you tell me how you really feel?" she says as she gets ready to knock a second loud-mouthed jerk on his butt today.

While she positions herself to deliver an impacting blow, a white sleeved arm with thick muscular hands swings Yuri around in the opposite direction. "I think the

Lady wants you to leave," Lt. Chris Rottanelli says. "But I want you to apologize to her first, and then maybe you'll leave in one piece."

Yuri scowls at the Coast Guard officer and says, "You sure you want to get that ice cream suit all bloody and messy, boy scout?" He throws a wild haymaker at Chris' face.

Chris shuffles very quickly inside Yuri's perimeter with his left foot first, blocks the punch with his left wrist, throws a very short powerful right straight punch to Yuri's sternum knocking the breath out of him, then wraps his right arm underneath Yuri's right shoulder while pulling his right arm forward with his left hand. At the same time, he puts his right foot inside Yuri's right instep while crouching down, pulls all Yuri's weight onto his hip, lifts him off the ground, and then with a violent twist slams Yuri to the pavement, at which point he puts him in a devastatingly painful wrist lock. Chris, always an intensely focused fighter, did not miss the fact that Danielle managed to grab Yuri's drink before it spilled onto his dress uniform.

"Now Mister, please apologize to the young lady."

"Yes, yes, of course. Danielle I am so sorry, please do not tell my uncle, I am a little drunk and am just angry that you will not go out with me."

"Oh, Yuri, don't worry, Uncle Boris will never know, and I will never forget what a fool you just made of yourself."

Yuri picks up what he has left of himself and his pride, and scampers away as fast as possible.

Danielle walks up to Chris, "Thanks for the help, cowboy, nice *seoi nage* throw. I like the short sternum punch setup too. But I could have handled Yuri myself."

"I am sure you could have Ms. Edwards, but I could not bear to see you mess up what I have to say is the most beautiful dress I have ever seen, and on such a stunningly beautiful woman."

Danielle blushes, places one hand on top the other in front of her and swoons as she says, "Sooo! You do know who I am and who my dad is don't you?"

"Yes of course I do. And by the way thanks for saving my uniform, Captain Phillips would have had my ass if I got it messed up here."

Danielle laughs a genuine and quite beautiful laugh. "You're welcome, Lieutenant."

"You don't remember me, do you Danielle?"

"What are you talking about, have we met?"

Chris recounts for her how he graduated from Manheim Township High School in Pennsylvania five years before she did and even worked one summer for her grandpa and dad, detailing cars.

"Oh my God, Christopher Rottanelli. You used to go by Christopher, right?"

"Oh, my mom always called me that, but once I got to Kings Point, I started going by Chris."

"Kings Point, huh?" Danielle says. "Did my dad talk you into that?"

Chris looks at Danielle. "Well, there's a lot more to it than that."

"Yes, I know, first you have to be nominated by an elected official and then one of the academies you apply to has to accept you. So how many did you apply to?"

"Just three; Naval, Coast Guard, and Kings Point. Kings Point wanted me, and there I went."

Danielle grabs Chris' hand and they start walking around the sign outside. "But you chose the Coast Guard."

"Well, yes, at Kings Point you get the Coast Guard license. The Coast Guard grads don't even get those right away. Great opportunity for advancement if they accept you from Kings Point."

Danielle is really enjoying talking to this guy. "That is exactly what Dad said he did. Say, I remember now. You were one of the best fighters at Nye's Gym back then. Boxing and kickboxing, right?"

"Yes, I did it all right there, but I did not have a man like your dad to train me at home."

"Well, being Jacob Edwards' daughter had its benefits."

"So you're down here with Chief Roberto and your grandmother, huh?"

"Yes, for now anyway. After the plane wreck, I just had to get away from Edwards Auto; too many memories there. But I love Grandpa, and everything about the business, and I do plan on going back someday, although he doubts it at times."

"You know that was one of the best summers of my life working in that shop. Tony was the boss, but your dad and Jim were always around and never thought twice about getting their hands dirty. I remember some

Thursday nights after a good day's work, your dad was back in the wash bay and Jim was out front inspecting and detailing every car until ten or eleven o'clock at night. Jim was always good for pizza, Kentucky Fried chicken, cheese steaks, or whatever the crew was into that night. Good times."

Danielle laughs, "Yeah, and I remember Mom yelling at Dad around midnight to take a shower before she would let him near their bed. Good times."

Danielle tells Chris about the '67 Mustang she started restoring earlier that day and invites him to come help if he has time. He says, "Well Brazos, is just a few miles away, maybe we could do that and then later go jet skiing or something."

"Why, Lt. Rottanelli, are you asking me out on a date?" Danielle asks.

Chris' cheeks turn beet red and he kind of stumbles over his words but manages to finally get out that as beautiful as she looks in that dress tonight, he'd be a complete idiot if he didn't.

She then grabs his hand and demurely takes him over to where Jim Edwards and Grandpa Roberto are talking. "Grandpas, I'd like you to meet Lieutenant Chris Rottanelli, who has just asked me out on a date this weekend, and before I say yes, I want both of your approvals."

Chris can hardly believe this. Both his cheeks are so hot now he thinks someone could fry an egg on them.

"Chief, Mr. Edwards," he says as he extends his hand to shake each of these very intimidating men's hands.

Roberto eyes him rather skeptically and begins to speak, but Jim pushes forward and gives Chris a big jovial hug, "Chris, by gawd, how have you been? I saw your mother at Roots Market the other day; she said you made full lieutenant recently. We sure are proud of you at the shop. Sure, you two kids go out and have a great time! If that's okay with you Roberto?"

Roberto switches gears as soon as he understands that this boy has been properly vetted by family and gives his consent as well.

Jim sticks his face in Danielle's ear and says, "Ouch, you really know how to scare a boy. Everyone knows how protective Roberto is about family and especially the females. Hell, your dad used to call me at night just to ask advice on how to talk to him whenever Mary would invite him over for dinner when they were dating."

Danielle just smiles, gives both her grandpas a big kiss and walks off escorted by this very intriguing and attractive young man.

Isabella comes up to her husband beaming from ear to ear and says loud enough for Jim to hear, "You know, Jacob walked around with that engagement ring in his pocket for almost four weeks trying to work up the courage to ask Mary to be his wife. I got so tired of waiting that I went out and bought her that dress for the annual Coast Guard Ball he took her to that year. Whew, one look at her in that thing standing on our front porch, that boy was on his knee, the ring was out, question asked, and popped on her finger like a flash."

Isabella snaps her finger. "Yup, Nana knows best. You remember Roberto, huh?"

Yeah, Nana knows best all right, Roberto thinks to himself, as he nods. Nana did not see that Russian creep Yuri hitting on Danielle either, nor the incident that followed. Although Roberto had to admit that this young Lieutenant was quite impressive, and reminded him of another young ensign that a beautiful Garcia girl caught the attention of not so many years ago. But be that as it may, he was still going to watch this just as closely, and make up his own mind.

CHAPTER FOUR
CLEANING UP MESSES

Back in Manheim, Same Night

In the back lot of Edwards Auto, Alan Rogers is cleaning his tools. Thursday nights are always late ones for him, but he is glad it is still warm at night so he can work outside, which really saves a lot of time. For Alan, time means money and Alan loves to make money. He pulls out the hundred bucks Boris gave him earlier to not work on the Camry and congratulates himself not only for the easy hundred, but the extra three hundred he made because he was able to fit in one of his own customers' cars.

Alan would never give up Edwards Auto as an account. Jim Edwards has him on a flat rate, so the most he can make on any given car was one hundred-fifty dollars, but honestly, that Camry of Jim's, oh yes, Boris', would have only been worth about seventy-five dollars work. What the hell—what they didn't know wouldn't hurt them.

Just then, he notices that at the end of the rod he is cleaning is a big chunk of black insulating tar. It was not uncommon to have a little bit of this stuff on the tools at the end of the day. Auto manufacturers use it to insulate panels for noise suppression and climate control. But this seems to be a lot and it is very gooey, almost like it hasn't even set up yet. As he pulls it off with the rag, he sees some green paper stuck inside the goo. He applies some lacquer thinner to the wad and cleans the goo off the paper. His jaw drops as he realizes he's holding the full top left-hand corner of a hundred-dollar bill. He wonders if there might be a stash of hundred-dollar bills where this came from. *Wow,* he thinks to himself, *maybe if I sneak over to Boris' part of the lot, I can find that Camry.*

As he stands up, he feels something go around his neck that is very thin and sharp.

Ivan pulls the homemade razor wire tourniquet violently around Alan's neck, slicing his windpipe, artery, and jugular vein at the same time. Blood shoots out in every direction as he lowers Alan's dying body to the pavement.

"You imbecile," is all Ivan hears before he feels a wooden cane crash down on the back of his head. He falls to the ground next to Alan's convulsing corpse. As Ivan turns, he sees Boris glaring at him with rage in his eyes that burns into his very soul. He begins to wonder if this parking lot will be the last thing he ever sees. Boris manages to take control of his rage and looks at the little pig of a shop foreman before him as he starts to sort out yet another mess Ivan has caused.

"I tell you to watch him, make sure he doesn't know anything. I leave for a few hours and find you here killing him right in front of our operation. Are you out of your mind?"

"I'm sorry Boris, but he found a piece of the American money we hid in the Camry and was going back to look for more. What was I to do?"

"For one, you little inbred Cossack, you were to call me immediately and I would have told you how to proceed." Boris looks at the scene before him with cold calculation that a lifetime of being one of the world's best assassins has afforded him, and begins to come up with a plan that may salvage this pig-headed situation.

He tells Ivan to take Alan's van and tools to their detail shop and to use only water and cleaning supplies found in the van to clean all of the blood off thoroughly, put everything back the way they found it, and call him when he is done so he can check the work. For the next part of his plan, Boris needs the kind of help that none of these idiots he's working with at his Manheim shop can provide. As Ivan drives off with Alan's van, Boris pulls out his cell phone and dials a number he never thought he would have to use while in Manheim. "Sal, my friend. How are you doing?"

"I can't complain, Boris. Are things going well in Manheim?"

"That is why I am calling you at this late hour, because things are not well In Manheim at all and I need your help immediately. No details right now, but please meet me at my business ASAP!"

Boris disconnects the line and puts the phone back in his pocket. Sal was not the best Boris had ever used in his former profession, but he was definitely the closest. Sal was a professional crime scene cleaner mostly used for organized crime in the Philadelphia area. Boris had used his team's services a few times in the past and kept Sal on a retainer. He also kept Sal apprised when he was in the area, just in case he would need his services.

Sal had been to the facility about a year ago to get his 2014 Cadillac Escalade fully detailed. Boris had insisted that Sal use Edwards Auto detailing service because he knew Ivan and the boys barely knew how to adequately wash a vehicle let alone detail it the way Edwards always did. Sal appreciated the job and gave a handsome tip to Tony and the crew over at Edwards when finished.

Sal lives in Reading, Pennsylvania. He drives fast, hoping to make it in about forty-five minutes. Tonight, he makes it in thirty-nine minutes. He and the two others he brought with him get briefed by Boris and then go to work on Alan and the scene. Boris thought he would kill two birds with one stone, so he instructed Sal to use the 2013 Red Toyota Camry he had hidden in his shop, the very one that his imbecilic shop foreman, Ivan, missed earlier that day when he grabbed Jim's Camry instead, to prep for sale and transport. For a little extra, Sal would dispose of the car and the body so that neither would ever be seen again.

As they meet in the shop, Boris tells Ivan to put the extra key in the car so all can be disposed. As Ivan retrieves the key and makes sure it is in the car, Sal and Boris say their goodbyes and head out. As usual, Boris has one of his own people follow Sal discreetly, to make sure all is done as he would wish. Boris did not get this far by leaving anything to chance. It was certainly to his advantage that Jim left earlier today on that Army transport plane out of Lancaster Airport to go be a part of the ceremony in South Texas, because that meant the only one who would be hanging around this late on a Thursday night before the sale would be him.

Foolish man, Jim, thought Boris. To think that he could sneak out of here without Boris knowing exactly what he was up to was absurd. He had been keeping a very close eye on the entire Edwards family for over fourteen years now, and he knows he will never let up until the job is completely finished and they are all gone. But he also knows there are a few more things that need to happen before that victorious day can be realized. Boris smiles and thinks that even with morons and imbeciles like his nephew Yuri, and his shop foreman Ivan, he, with his sniper-bred patience, is on the verge of a multi-billion dollar empire that will put him at the head of all money laundering for organized crime on the entire East Coast, and someday the West Coast as well. He smiles, enjoying the thoughts of his soon-to-be success as he lights his expensive Cuban cigar and walks back to his shop to inspect Ivan's work on Alan's van.

Four Years After Cozumel, Edwards Auto, Office of Vice President Jacob Edwards

"Bzzzzzzz."

"Jacob, you have a Chuck Yeager out here from the FBI who wants to speak with you."

"Chuck?" Jacob's eyes light up. "Holy shit, send him in."

Charles Seymour Yeager, Jacob thinks as a very jovial and handsome middle-aged man walks into Jacob's office with a huge smile and both arms stretched out ready to embrace his old Kings Point roommate.

"Chuck, my God, it has been too long."

Chuck releases himself from one of Jacob's famous bear hugs and just looks his old friend in the eye. "Good gawd, man. You're stronger now than when we were at Kings Point."

"Well, I have Danielle keeping me on my toes. At this place you cannot show weakness to Dad or the troops, or they will eat you alive."

"Oh sure," says Chuck. "And no one is afraid of being tossed off a building or something?"

"Hey, buddy, I only use that move for one offence and it hasn't happened here."

"Yes," says Chuck. "After what you and I found in that cabin on that yacht down off Honduras back in '96, I don't blame you one bit for Cozumel."

Jacob pauses for a moment as an old painful memory momentarily resurfaces, then sits and says. "Ancient history my friend. What brings you here?"

"Well you're not going to like it, but the whole Cozumel thing has caught the attention of the FBI."

"Oh, for crying out loud! Can't they just let sleeping dogs lie, Chuck? This thing has been hashed out a hundred times. Can't I just get on with my life?"

"Sure, Jacob, but some evidence turned up that has everyone in my unit scratching their heads."

"Oh yeah," says Jacob. "Like what?"

"Well for starters," Chuck says as he sits, "those three shots that your report says came at you from the cutter—"

"Phillips and I both decided it had to have come from the cutter," Jacob interjects, "because they were straight in front of us and attempting to flee."

"Yeah, but the trajectory does not match up with the positioning of the ships at the time. Now, you know Admiral Harrington just retired this year and we come to find out that he did not pursue any of this in his investigation. It was like he wanted to get rid of the incident as fast as possible."

Jacob shakes his head. "That old blowhard did not like me one bit. "He thought his son, Will, should have been given command of *First Responder*, and blamed me for taking it away from him. But I think the commandant and the Secretary of Homeland Security kind of pushed to get rid of the thing as well. The president did not want any more strained relations with Mexico, so they did not want Harrington digging up anything else that might incriminate me, and that might make them all look bad. So, what about the trajectory?" Jacob says with a hint of sarcasm.

"The angle of the impact does not line up with where the cutter was positioned at the time the shots were fired."

"What does it line up with then?"

Chuck looks Jacob straight in the eye and says, "The cruise ship."

"What the fuck? You've got to be kidding me, right? The NSA vetted every one of those pirates and there was no one in that bunch that could even come close to making a shot like that. Hell, that cruise ship was almost a half mile away when those shots came."

"Correction, they vetted everyone that stayed, but you are forgetting about that high-powered speed yacht that got away."

"Wow, did anyone ever figure out what the hell that was?"

"Well, whatever it was, it's way above a Caribbean pirate's pay grade. Our theory is that it was some kind of souped-up Sun Ark with military grade radar jamming and stealth technology."

"Geez, Chuck. Pirates don't have that kind of loot. What the hell was going on?"

"Well, for starters, outside of the dead people on the cruise ship, only three are unaccounted for—the nanny, an older Russian man, and his young girlfriend."

"I knew about the nanny; she took care of President Gonzales' daughters. But who is the Russian and his girlfriend?"

"That is the big mystery, Jacob. None of these people ever turned up again. The Russian was on the ship with an alias and so was the girl. People do it all the time to avoid publicity, especially rich old men who want to get away with their girlfriends. The only thing we all were waiting for was some kind of ransom demand coming up so we could identify the guy."

"So what has all this to do with the sniper fire?"

"The three slugs that were dug out of your old cutter were 7.62x54mmR rounds from an SV-98."

"Shit," says Jacob.

"High-powered Russian sniper rifle, shot by an obvious expert." Chuck looks at his friend sternly and replies, "It makes perfect sense. No sniper is going to want to take a shot like that on board a cutter on high seas in combat."

"Yes, Chuck, I get it, a stabilized cruise ship would be a much more ideal platform. Where do you think the shot was taken from on the ship?"

"That's the real clicker in all this. It was from one of the luxury suites on the same side of the ship that our Russian and his girlfriend were staying."

"So what is your point, Chuck?"

"Well, Jacob, one working theory is that *you* were the target all along."

Jacob is visibly shocked. "Me! Who the hell would want to kill me? I don't know any Russian secret agents. My name isn't James Bond you know."

"We are still working this all out. There is one more tidbit of info you might find interesting, though."

"Yeah, what's that?"

"Marnia Gonzales, the girl you saved, just came out and said her father was having an affair with the nanny right up to the time of the hijacking."

"Geez, Chuck. This is sounding a little too saucy for me. That's why I chose command and you kept on with investigative law enforcement."

Chuck gives Jacob the thumbs up and says, "Well anyway, buddy, we're keeping an eye on things and that includes you and yours for the time being."

"Well that just makes me feel like a little baby all safe and snug sucking on mama Chuck's tit."

"Oh, shut up you asshole. Well, I have to get back to Philadelphia."

"Philadelphia, huh? You know Danielle and Mary have been looking at Temple University. I will expect you to keep my little girl safe while she's there."

"Huh, from what I hear, and knowing her father, it's Philadelphia that needs the protection."

"Yeah, whatever. Nice talking to you, buddy. You go get those bad guys. I am going to help my dad unload nine hundred and seventy-six units tomorrow, and then go to the lake with the family."

"Okay. See you Jacob. Do call if anything comes up, and I will be in touch."

"Oh sure. If some Russian James Bond shows up, you'll be the first to know."

They both shake hands and Chuck walks out of Jacob's office thinking it sure is good to see him so happy. Jacob was one of the most dedicated Coast Guard officers that Chuck had ever known. But anyone who really knew him also knew where he belonged and it was right here with his dad kicking ass at the auction. He really thought Jacob would have walked away at eight years of service after what they saw down in Honduras on that yacht.

They were both junior lieutenants when their skipper ordered them to take a skiff over and investigate the luxury boat one mile out from the nearest port. Jacob, Chuck, and two crewmen went over. Jacob was first through the door into the lounge, and what he found would haunt both of them for the rest of their lives—an entire family butchered and lying all over the place. The worst was in the back room. They found a thirteen-year-old girl brutally beaten, raped, and bloody, her face so swollen you could not see her eyes. All of her clothes were ripped off and she was curled up in a corner, bleeding, sobbing, and dying.

Jacob grabbed a fresh blanket and covered her up while Chuck called for medevac. Jacob held and rocked the little girl in his arms. He tried to soothe her in any way he could. She was so far gone she could hardly speak, but three words were barely audible as he cradled her, "*Donde esta mi mama?*" —"Where is my mother?"

She died in Jacob's arms that day, and in a way, something died in Jacob as well. He really did not start to recover from the shock until the birth of his own daughter Danielle later that year.

Yes, Chuck knew exactly why Commander Jacob Edwards threw that piece-of-shit pirate off that cruise ship observation deck that day and did not blame him one bit. He would have done the same himself, given the chance.

"Pardon me, but could you tell me where to find Jim Edwards please?" Chuck looks up to see a rather distinguished older Russian man, probably in his early to mid-sixties, standing before him with a very expensive Cuban cigar in his hand. "My name is Boris and I am a client of Jim's, so could you please direct me to his whereabouts?"

"Oh," says Chuck. "Uh, I don't work here but Jim's son, Jacob, is in his office. I am sure he can help you."

"Thank you," says Boris as he turns almost right into Jacob coming out of his office.

"Boris, Dad's around back in the detailing bay getting his hands dirty. I am heading to the wash bay to get some work done. If you want to talk, you'll have to go into the shop."

"Oh, that is quite all right, Jacob. I will wait until he is done, thank you."

Jacob chuckles, "Suit yourself, Boris."

"Good seeing you Chuck. Have fun in Philly being an FBI bad-guy hunter. I am going to go wash some cars."

"See you Jacob," he says then looks at Boris. "And nice to meet you Boris." Chuck thinks to himself, *Jacob doesn't like that guy very much. He must be a real creep. Jacob has always been a great judge of character.*

As Chuck drives away, Boris says to himself, "Jacob now you are talking to the FBI. I wonder what that is all about."

Present Day, Friday, Late Afternoon after the Sale

Boris is sitting at a table in the cafeteria of the Manheim Auto Auction, going over the paperwork for the cars he has sold that day on lane nineteen. He learned a few years ago to not appear too prosperous in his auctioning off of the vehicles. Suspicion, in any way, was not something Boris wanted to promote when it came to his dealings at the auction. Many times, he had to make sure that his online bidders did not appear too anxious and overzealous in their acquisitions. Paying too much "stupid money" as the other wholesalers called it would only bring undue attention to his operation.

He feels a hand on his shoulder and sees it is Jim Edwards with the same question in his eyes he always has at the end of a sale day.

"I just barely did seventy percent today," he answers the unspoken question with a slight smirk.

"Well, everybody has an off week, even in the middle of summer, Boris. Better luck next week. If you would get CR's and try other lanes, you might have done eighty-seven percent like we did today, highest average so far today, buddy. Someday you're going to listen to me, huh?"

Boris puts on his best hurt look and says, "Why do you rub it in every time you do better than me, Jim?"

Jim laughs and slaps him on the back and tells him he's one of his best clients and that he just wants to help him do better. Boris thanks him. He can't help himself from pointing out that Jim looks kind of tired today, knowing full well that the army transport plane that brought him back from the grand opening of Roberto's ridiculous restaurant did not land him in Lancaster until 5 a.m. that morning.

Jim tells him he was up late last night inspecting inventory.

As Jim walks away, Boris thinks that if he *had* been doing that last night he might not be breathing today. As he stands to leave the cafeteria table he is sitting at, the man that he sent to spy on Sal comes into the cafeteria from the side entrance, and motions Boris to the large hallway by the operations desk outside. Boris leaves his lunch tray on the table and packs up his briefcases and joins him.

"What is your report?" he says to the burly Russian man before him.

"I followed Sal into Philadelphia and he went directly to your mafia client Arthur Mancini's dock and met with him."

Boris had been taking care of laundering Mr. Mancini's money for several years now. Though he knew Arthur to be ambitious, he never considered him a threat until now.

"Were you able to hear the conversation?" Boris asks as he lights a cigar.

"Of course," says his man, and he begins to unfold that he found Sal and Arthur talking on the docks about the dead PDR guy and red Toyota Camry that Sal was supposed to dispose of.

"So, Arthur tells Sal that they can use it as leverage against you in getting in on your money laundering operation. He says all the crime families on the East Coast have been taking note of your very dramatic rise to power in the last decade. He tells Sal, 'No one has been able to match Boris' price for money laundering. All the other competitors are paid fifty to sixty cents on the dollar for laundered money, but Boris' scheme has been paying eighty-five cents on the dollar. Over ninety percent of the crime syndicates on the East Coast are already using Boris, and it looks like the West Coast is starting to get interested in him as well.' Arthur tells Sal that it could be a two billion dollar per year business and he wants in. He had Sal leave the car and the body with him stored in a container on the docks. I have our people watching. It has not moved yet."

"This is unfortunate for Arthur and Sal, my friend. Keep watching that container. I will deal with them both tonight," Boris says as he flings his half-smoked cigar into the nearest ashtray, wraps up his paper work, and leaves the building in somewhat of a rush.

That evening, Sal is sitting by the window in his home on the outskirts of Reading, Pennsylvania, drinking a glass of wine and looking at the news. It is a hot summer night in southern Pennsylvania and Boris is glad that Sal has his window open because there won't be any sound of broken glass when he puts a bullet in the head of this traitorous Cossack. He takes careful aim and waits for Sal's head to be positioned for the perfect shot.

Sal thinks about how good it's going to be when he can start getting his piece of that two billion per year business Arthur was talking about last night. It's the last thought he will ever think. Boris squeezes the trigger of his silenced sniper rifle and Sal falls forward in his chair, dead instantly.

Later that evening, Arthur Mancini is shot in the head after he pulls into the parking garage of his downtown penthouse apartment. The bodies are discovered the next morning, giving Boris and his associates plenty of time to find and dispose of the bothersome red Toyota and the body of Alan the PDR guy. They decide to keep everything in the storage container. Boris believes he is wise when he has several holes put into side of the container so that it will quickly fill with water. They load it onto a garbage barge and take it out into the bay where they drop it over the side down to the ocean floor.

On his drive back to Manheim, Boris can't help but think that none of this would have happened if his idiot shop foreman had not grabbed one of Jim's cars by mistake and already prepped and loaded it for delivery. He was going to have to make some adjustments in the command structure of his organization to avoid future mishaps such as this. He was stuck having to put up with his dense nephew Yuri, or nothing would work, but everyone else's position was subject to change.

CHAPTER FIVE
CHIVALRY IS NOT DEAD

Saturday Morning, South Texas

Saturday mornings were Danielle's "me time", usually. She could sleep in, go for a run, catch up on all her favorite shows—using Grandpa's online video streaming accounts, of course. But today is special. She's going on the first date she's had in over three years, and with a very intriguing young man. Chris is picking her up at nine and they are heading over to Juan's house to work on the Mustang. Instead of jet skiing they decided to go horseback riding on Padre Island, close to Station Brazos.

Danielle can hardly contain herself. She wants everything to be perfect. What to wear? What to wear?

She panics a bit knowing that Chris is going to be there any minute. She is frantically painting her nails when a knock sounds at the front door of her efficiency. She practically falls over backward as she jumps out of her chair. "Oh my God," she says to herself. He's just going to have to wait outside until I am dressed.

She steps up to the door and opens it with her best put-on smile, "Chris, you're early! I'm not even halfway done getting ready. You're going to have to wait outside, I live in an efficiency apartment and I can't invite you in."

"What are you talking about getting ready?" Chris laughs. "I thought we were going over to your dance student's home to help restore a very cool 1967 Ford Mustang."

Danielle gulps and then takes a closer look at Chris. He is wearing some old jeans, and a short sleeve work shirt that says "Edwards Auto" on it.

Chris laughs. "You're wearing blue jeans and a tee-shirt too. Let's just go. We can change later for riding at the stable yard. They have his and her showers and a changing room right there."

Danielle gulps down about a ton of embarrassment as she walks over to her dresser. She pulls out her riding clothes and boots and puts them in a bag. She goes over to her closet, reaches inside a storage box, and pulls out her own Edwards Auto work shirt that just so happens to be a different color than Chris' because it is the color that the managers wear. It has her first name and title, "Assistant Vice President".

Chris stares at her with a wry smile and says, "Okay boss. You ready to go?"

She walks in front of Chris towards the door and says over her shoulder, "Sure am. Now let's get some work done today. Okay Rottanelli?"

"Yes Ma'am," he says as he follows her out to his car. All the time, he's thinking to himself, *boy, do those jeans look nice on her.*

They pull up to Miguel and Juan's house just before 9 a.m. Both of them are already out front with the Mustang and a big engine hoist that Miguel rented the previous evening. Chris and Danielle get out of his little Jeep Wrangler. She didn't want Grandpa Roberto to take the Skylark away from her for getting it dirty again. He threatened to make her drive her uncle's 1979 Ford Pinto that he had in storage if he ever again saw the Skylark as messy as it was the night of the grand opening of Jacob's Ladder. Danielle would rather walk than to allow herself to be humiliated by driving a Pinto, but it really wasn't practical to have to walk to work and dance class. Taking the Jeep to Miguel's was the perfect solution.

"Whew, you weren't just blowing hot air when you said this is a work of art. Man, what a machine," Chris says as his eyes devour the magnificent piece of automotive history before him. Chris could tell that the trio pretty much had the car ready for the body shop and the paint job that was going to bring this beast back to life again.

Miguel begins to move the engine hoist into place as he says, "I still do not understand why we have to take the engine out before we take it to the body shop, Danielle. There is no rust in the engine well and I am a very good mechanic. I completely tested the engine out last night and it runs great."

Danielle looks at Chris and asks him if he remembers Pete, the auto wholesaler who was always trying to do restorations and sell them in the big Spring Classic Sale at Manheim.

"Oh yeah, the tall lanky guy who never wanted to finish the job."

Danielle makes the point that he always missed bringing a classic car back to life in two areas—engine wells and trunks. She explains that one time he had a 1964 Cadillac Eldorado convertible. Everyone was so excited to get that baby ready. Pete had them do a complete restoration to the interior, give it a new paint job, and even had the spoke wheels rechromed, but when Grandpa tried to get him to do the trunk and engine compartment, he refused citing that he already put about six thousand dollars into the restoration and he did not want to spend anymore. So they took that Eldorado to the spring sale that year and ran it in the GM classic lane. There were two other '64 Eldorados that went through that lane that day almost identical to Pete's. One sold for thirty-four thousand, and the other for thirty-eight thousand. Pete's sold for a mere eleven thousand. He barely broke even on the car.

"You see, Miguel," says Danielle, "when it comes to getting top dollar for a classic car, you have to go all the way. Pete missed out on a twenty thousand dollar or more profit because he just didn't listen to Grandpa. When these kinds of buyers look at cars, they want to open the hood and the trunk and see pure factory perfection—and when I say factory, I mean all stock. The more original, the higher the bid. The Cadillac that did four thousand less than the other did so because the owner put some fancy aftermarket custom wheels on it and the other had restored stock."

Chris marvels at Danielle's passion for all things cars. "My God, Danielle," he exclaims, "listening to you talk about cars is like listening to your dad talk. You really love this stuff. That's amazing."

"Thanks for the compliment," she says.

Miguel concedes to Danielle's logic and proceeds to unmount the Ford small-block 289 engine from the engine well. Then Juan begins to sand and prep the well for paint. Danielle puts Chris in charge of the trunk doing the same thing. She and Miguel get started taking the seats, door panels, dash, carpet, and headliner out. They dust, lightly sand, and prep the interior of the Mustang while also thoroughly cleaning, shampooing, and polishing everything. She is pleased to see that after cleaning the vinyl and leather, they will have to do very little dyeing. Miguel did a pretty decent job of storing his father's car.

They put in six hours of hard work when the tow truck arrives to take the Mustang to the body shop. Danielle already left detailed instructions on how she wants the car painted, and said that she would be by on Monday to check on the progress. The four of them put all the spare parts, including the engine, into the barn for safe keeping.

"Now you need to rent a hot water pressure washer this week so we can steam this engine down, acid clean the block, and repaint the headers and the air filter cover, okay?" Danielle instructs Miguel.

Juan pipes in to exclaim, "I found some really nice chrome valve and air filter covers online that would look really smoking, Danielle."

She points her finger and shoots back, "No aftermarket Juan, only stock parts."

Juan concedes and mumbles something about not wanting to be a Pete repeat.

Chris and Danielle say goodbye to Juan and his dad, and head to the horse stables on Padre Island over by station Brazos.

"Man, that was so much fun," Chris says as he looks at Danielle's very cute and dirty face.

Danielle sighs, puts both hands behind her bushy blond hair and says, "Yes sometimes I forget how much I love this stuff. Not just working on them but thinking all the nuts and bolts through, getting them ready, getting them to market, selling them. It's such a thrill. Daddy, Grandpa, and I had so much fun. It never seemed like work. We were one kick-ass team."

All of a sudden, she starts to cry.

Chris pulls the Jeep off the road, and puts his hand on her back as she cradles her head in her lap.

"Chris, I miss them so much. Sometimes I feel like this is all fake, that they can't be dead. We were so happy, the five of us, at Edwards Auto, working together. All I ever wanted to do was help Grandpa and Daddy build that business to be the best in the world. Mom and Grandma loved that I was so into it. Going to college all that studying, business, economics, accounting, it was all for that. That's why I worked so hard because I wanted it. I really did. I guess I thought we would all just go on forever being with each other and doing what we love. Now it's all blown up, all gone."

"It's not all gone, Danielle. Jim's still there," Chris says with a big lump in his throat, as he realizes he's about to cry himself.

Danielle sees the beginning of tears in Chris' eyes and lays her head on his chest as he puts his arm around her.

"I know. I know, I need to be with him, but I needed family. I needed time to think. Grandpa and Nana have such a huge wonderful family down here. I wanted Grandpa Jim to come with me but he couldn't. He said Daddy would not have approved at all. He would have said that his place was there, and that he had over a hundred people depending on him and they all had families too. He knew Grandpa Roberto would take care of me just as good as he would, so he let me go. He told me he loved me, and that it was all mine anytime I wanted it."

Chris holds Danielle a little closer and says in her ear, "Besides your dad, there has only ever been one other person that could run that place with the kind of love and fire that Jim Edwards has, and that's you, Danielle.

I believe that with all my heart. Your grandpa is the toughest old guy I have ever known and he will wait until you are ready, even if that's not until he's a hundred years old, he'll wait."

"I know that, Chris. He's just a big old teddy bear with me, and I love him with everything I have. It's just not the same anymore without Mom and Grandma. They kept Grandpa and Daddy in line. They made sure that family came before business no matter what. They were a couple of iron maidens when it came to family. I don't know what to do with Grandpa since the accident. He's turned into a hermit. He closed up that beautiful house he and Grandma lived in and rented that ridiculous little log cabin up behind Myers Furniture, which he basically just sleeps in except on Sundays when he sits around in his underwear all day watching old movies."

"Sounds like he needs another iron maiden to keep him in line," Chris says. "Does he date or anything these days?"

Danielle gasps, "Oh my God, no. Grandpa was, is, and always will be a one-woman man and nothing is ever going to change that. That's another thing. I don't want to just take care of Grandpa and run his business for the rest of my life. I want to get married someday and have a family of my own, you know," she says as she looks deeply into Chris' eyes, which, to his surprise, does not scare, but deeply excites him.

Chris gulps and gathers himself as he says, "Danielle Edwards, I have been around your family for a while now and if there is one thing that I will vouch for it is this; there is nothing that an Edwards can't do if they want too. Multitasking is in your genetic makeup. We all carry our families inside of us in one way or another and you definitely have some very appealing qualities in you that come from everyone you're related too. Don't sell yourself short. If Danielle Edwards wants to do something, God save the poor sorry S.O.B. that tries to stop her."

Danielle sighs and buries her head deeper into Chris' chest as she thinks to herself what an amazing guy this Lt. Chris Rottanelli of the United States Coast Guard is.

The rest of the day unfolds like a beautiful dream for Danielle. They arrive at the horse rental around 4 p.m. It is a beautiful summer day on Padre Island—perfect for horseback riding and picnicking. They use the showers at the facility to clean up and change out of their Mustang restoration clothing, and head out into the beautiful afternoon.

Chris finds the perfect place to stop and eat. They sit in the early evening looking out at the Gulf waters gently slapping up against the rocky cliff walls below them. The horses are tethered to a nearby pole near a water-filled basin for them to drink. A gentle and warm breeze comes over the waters as they turn around and watch the sun set over the Texas–Mexico horizon. Danielle lies against Chris' chest as she looks up and says, "My dad used to bring Mother and me outside on nights like this when we lived down here when I was little. He loved watching these sunsets while cradling us in his arms."

They return the horses a little late, which costs Chris more money, but he easily justifies it. They drive back to Danielle's apartment in a very relaxing and endearing quiet. Danielle cannot help herself. She just keeps staring at Chris while he drives. He occasionally looks over at her and says, "What?" as he shrugs his shoulders and they both start laughing.

When they get to Danielle's place, Chris walks her to the door and they stand and look at each other a little nervously but excited at the same time. Finally, Chris gently pulls Danielle to him and kisses her in a soft, almost delicate way that Danielle then returns with a little more passion and fire. The kiss is something fantastic to both of them and neither wants to stop but Chris finally pulls back to say, "Good night, Danielle. This has been a very special day for me."

Danielle says it has been wonderful for her as well, and then before she can stop the words from coming out of her mouth, she asks him if he would like to come in and stay the night with her.

Chris smiles and looks Danielle in the eye and says, "Danielle, at this moment there is nothing in this world I want more. But I just had the best date of my life with the most beautiful girl I have ever known, and I want to have hundreds more just like it with that girl. You're the girl I want to take home and show off to my parents. You're the girl I want to take to the annual ball this winter, and you're the girl I want to try to build something with. So with all my heart I am saying no. Not yet. I hope you understand?"

Tears just start streaming down Danielle's face as she grabs Chris and holds him with all her might. They kiss once more, and Chris turns and walks back to his Jeep mumbling to himself, "Thank God she didn't wear that dress today."

Danielle opens her apartment door and floats inside. About five minutes later her phone rings and it's her nana. "Hi Nana, how are you?"

Nana just laughs and says, "So Danielle, how was your date?"

Danielle's response is an explosion, "Oh my God, Nana, it was the most wonderful time I have ever had. He is such a great guy, and what a gentleman! I can't believe we lived in the same area so long while I was growing up. I know he is five years older than me, but I should have gotten to know him better back then…"

They talk so late into the night that Grandpa Roberto finally has to order Isabella off the phone to go to bed.

Before she hangs up, Danielle says, "Oh Nana, I think I'll come to Bible study at your house tomorrow morning, okay?"

"Oh Danielle, that will be wonderful. I'll tell Grandpa Roberto. *Amor* darling, good night."

Sunday Morning, Manheim

Jim loves his Sundays. It really is his day of rest. Outside of going to the gym for a thirty-minute express workout, he just sits around his little log cabin man cave and watches old classic movies in his shorts and a tee-shirt. He is deeply into *McClintock*, one of his favorite John Wayne movies, watching his favorite scene where

McClintock is keeping an irate father from killing an Indian for a crime he did not commit. Jim's blood starts pumping as John Wayne pushes the pilgrim back with his own shotgun and says, "…somebody ought to punch you straight in the mouth but I won't, I won't—the hell I won't," and he punches the guy so hard he flies down the hill and into a muddy pond at the bottom.

Jim yells, "Yeah!" as he thinks to himself, *there just aren't very many men around like that these days.* Then he thinks again. *Yes, but Jacob was a man like that.*

He hears a knock at the front door, about six feet from where he is sitting. "Who is it?" he yells as he stands to put a robe on.

"It's Barbara. You forgot to sign the paperwork for Boris' cars being taken down to South Texas for holding and shipment into Mexico."

Jim opens up the door and there in front of him stands the very sultry and beautifully dressed Barbara. Today she is wearing a very tight v-neck, low-cut white dress, which doesn't hesitate to show off her very ample breasts and beautiful tan legs. Barbara came to Edwards Auto just after the accident. She was from Honduras, but spoke very fluent English and had a Masters in Business Administration from a college in Russia, of all places. Boris had recommended her for the job of office manager after Linda was lost in the plane accident. She had proven to be very good at two things—doing a superb job with Edwards Auto's bookkeeping and management, and making Jim as uncomfortable as hell with her constant flirtation. Jim was going to be seventy this year and Barbara had to be somewhere around forty. Jim had learned a long time ago never to ask a woman her age, so he really did not know for sure.

"I am sorry, Barbara. It looks like you are all dressed up to go to, uh, church or something and instead, I have you working."

"Oh Jim, you are such a big teddy bear. I just had a few things to catch up on at the office, and then I'm heading to the country club to play a few rounds of golf."

"Barbara, if you try swinging a golf club in that dress out there, and in those heels, there won't be a man on that entire course who will be able to concentrate. If they are with their wives, they are going to get a club bent over their heads for looking at you!" Jim says as he grabs the paper work and brings it to his little kitchen table to sign.

Barbara walks over to the table and puts her hand on Jim's chest. "Perhaps if I had a handsome gentleman with me, my honor would be protected."

Jim lets out a big old breath and looks at this woman who is about the same age as his son's wife was at the time of the plane wreck. "Barbara, why do you want to waste your efforts on an old dog like me? There is hardly a man in Manheim who wouldn't sell his soul to have a shot at you, but here you are coming on to this old grandpa."

Barbara grabs the paperwork and seductively turns toward the door, strategically brushing her hips against the outside of Jim's left thigh as she says, "Why Jim, where I grew up it is quite common for older gentlemen to have a young and beautiful woman."

Jim stutters and says, "I know Barbara, and I am very flattered and a little astonished at all this attention you're giving me, but my heart will always belong to Linda, and that is just that. I spent almost fifty years building a life with that woman and I have to be honest, I just don't have it in me to do it with anyone else. I will tell you this though, when I go to the gym today, I am going to run circles around all those other people in the thirty-minute express workout area, because I think you got this old man's pulse up past two hundred."

Barbara can't help herself. She turns to look at Jim and chuckles with a genuine affection and respect for this old hermit.

"You know Jim, I should be insulted, but you restore my confidence in the human race. I hope there are more men like you around because I have not met many of them at all." Barbara tucks the documents under her arm and heads out the front door.

Alone again, Jim picks up a picture of his son in his dress-white Coast Guard uniform and says to himself, "Well I know of one who was better than me, little girl." He puts his lukewarm coffee into the microwave, heats it up, presses the play button on his Comcast remote, and continues his movie. "I think I'll get to the gym earlier today."

Barbara gets into her BMW 535i Sedan and drives back to Edwards Auto to make sure the papers get to the customs office in South Texas in time. As she pulls up, Boris is waiting for her outside in the parking lot.

"Did you get the documents ready, Barbara?"

"Yes, I am going in to notarize them and send them immediately," she says with a little fear and loathing at the same time.

"And how is our friend Jim responding to your flirtations so far? Hopefully you have at least seduced him by now. We need, as they say here in America, to make him think with the wrong head."

Barbara is annoyed at this point as she shoots back, "No Boris. I have not slept with Jim Edwards yet and I sincerely doubt that I ever will."

Boris steps in very close to her and puts a threatening heavy hand under her chin, wrapping his fingers around her throat. "Barbara, Barbara, Barbara. My dear, how can a woman who seduced and manipulated the great *Presidente* Gonzalez of Mexico find it so difficult to seduce some old cowboy from Wyoming?"

Barbara is defiant and stern as she almost spits in Boris' face and says, "That old cowboy is still in love with his dead wife and finds it a little sleazy to be messing around with a woman way younger than he is. For God's sake Boris, don't you get these people yet? Jim's a family man and cannot be manipulated like Gonzalez. The president of Mexico had an ego the size of the Mediterranean and that made it easy to play on his vanities." She reaches up and yanks Boris' hand from her throat and sticks her finger in his chest. "Never forget that it was me who got the whole Mexican customs' offices to work with you and your little scheme, and also me who used Gonzales' secrets to manipulate cartel involvement and protection. Don't ever even pretend to threaten me again Boris. Everything you are, everything you have done, is all up here," she says as she taps the front of her head. "Now, excuse me, please, I have work to do." She turns and storms off into the Edwards Auto main office building.

Boris smirks a little, lights his Cuban cigar, and sighs to himself while thinking Barbara has been most instrumental for a long time. She may know almost as much as he about this operation, but one bullet between the eyes can erase all that information. Boris walks back to his latest pimped-out Hummer thinking his SV-98 sniper rifle has been his truest and most reliable friend. It has seldom let him down, and when it does, he knows the fault is his own. He knows how to correct others. He simply has to eliminate. "Don't fail me, Barbara or you too will be introduced to my one true and dearest friend." Boris drives away.

Barbara slams the outside door behind her and turns to lock it as Boris drives off. She knows she took a big chance standing up to him like that, but the fact that Jim Edwards could resist her charms was somehow empowering her. The number of men she has manipulated over twenty years for that snake Boris is enough to turn her stomach inside out. All she's ever wanted is to be back home with Mama and Papa in their little cottage by the sea in Honduras. Her papa was a semi-successful tug boat operator at the docks, and she just loved to help him take care of his boat. Life was so peaceful and wonderful back then.

They were such a happy family. All they had to do that day was go out and help that rich family with their yacht. The finance minister and his wife had forgotten some provisions for their trip to Argentina and wanted Papa to bring it out to them. She and Papa were aboard the yacht when the pirate boat attacked. She can still remember the Jamaican man with the long braided hair telling his men that Barbara would be his first plaything, and that they could have the rest of the family in the cabin. Papa tried to defend her, but the man with the braided hair was a great fighter. He easily defeated Papa and threw him overboard, then he turned his attention back to her. As he was ready to grab her, they both turned at the sound of a foghorn to see another very large and much more luxurious yacht approaching.

It was dark gray with a sinister aura around the vessel. A distinguished looking foreign man, Boris, was standing on the deck asking the braided-hair Jamaican if he had killed the minister yet and had gotten the documents out of his safe. The Jamaican yelled back that everything was going as planned, but the foreigner on the yacht was not convinced. The bigger yacht docked with the smaller, and Boris told his men to fish the tug boat operator out of the ocean as he came aboard.

"Leave her alone, you disgusting pig. I told you that all the family would be yours, but she is not part of this family and therefore not part of the deal."

The Jamaican defiantly shot back, "All the women on this boat are mine, you Russian swine."

Boris took his walking stick and cracked the Jamaican in the knee so hard that he fell to the deck, screaming in agony. He pulled a long, narrow razor-sharp blade from inside the cane and leveled it at the Jamaicans throat. "Did your people not tell you that I am not one to be trifled with?"

The angry Jamaican was not stupid enough to make any defense. He had been well versed in who this man was and what he was capable of, so he asked for forgiveness and then headed to the cabin to finish the job that he was sent to do.

The men made quick work of the minister and his wife, but not before they made the minister open his safe. The Jamaican brought the desired package to Boris who was satisfied with the contents and then turned his attention to the beautiful young woman in front of him. "You are a very beautiful young woman, and so very alluring indeed. Such raw talent to distract my men from doing their jobs. I think I can put your talents to very good use. Put her and her father on board and secure them. I will be over shortly."

Boris looked at the Jamaican and said, "Do what you want to with the rest of the family, but then destroy this boat and leave no evidence that we were ever here."

"Yes," the Jamaican eagerly agreed, "It will be my pleasure."

The Jamaican heard something delightfully alluring coming from the bedroom behind the main cabin. There, he found one of the teenage daughters of the minister, hiding in the closet. The Jamaican smiled and counted his blessings, thanking whatever demons had provided for his needs.

Boris boarded his boat with his two new captives and their tug boat in tow. In one sense he had saved her—but what for, a life like this?

What a horrible memory. Barbara's remorse runs deep. She still suffers from the guilt of having anything to do with the deaths of that poor family. Boris' boat took her and her papa to this version of hell that she had been living in for some twenty years now. She remembers hearing that the Jamaican was never able to destroy the minister's yacht because a United States Coast Guard patrol boat showed up about an hour later, and the Jamaican and his crew had to leave quickly or be caught. "Someday," Barbara promised herself, "my papa and I will be free of you Boris. Someday."

Same Morning, South Texas

Danielle awakens feeling like a fairytale princess with a pretty good Prince Charming candidate on her mind. Usually on Sunday mornings, she would get up and go for a run. But this morning, she feels like dancing, so she goes to the studio at 7 a.m. and enjoys rehearsing her favorite scenes from her upcoming recital. Somehow, dancing to *"A Better Place"* by Rachel Platten seems like the right thing to do this morning, and Danielle always trusts her instincts.

At 9 a.m. her cell phone rings and to her delight, it is Chris. "Good morning, Lieutenant Rottanelli, to what do I owe the pleasure of hearing from you so soon?"

Chris laughs and says, "What do you mean so soon? It's been almost ten hours since I've seen you. What do you have planned for today?" he asks a little anxiously.

Danielle puts her index finger to her chin like she has to think and says, "Well, for starters, I am about to head over to Grandpa Roberto's and Nana's house for a home Bible fellowship meeting. And this afternoon, I don't really know".

Chris' curiosity is piqued as he says, "Chief Roberto does a home Bible fellowship? Is that like the Amish in Lancaster County?"

"Not quite. I have been going almost every Sunday, and Grandpa Roberto is a very dynamic Bible teacher. He and Nana have been involved with a group for almost eight years now. They have taken several classes and about three years ago were asked to take on a home fellowship in this area."

"Wow," says Chris. "If Chief Roberto is doing something like that, I really want to check it out. Can I come with you?"

Now Danielle gets really excited because she knows how much this is going thrill her Nana. "Sure! Come pick me up and we'll go together."

Okay," says Chris. "But can we take the '72 Skylark instead of my Jeep? I could drive it, if you don't want to," he hopefully adds.

"Don't push your luck, Chris. We will take Grandpa's Skylark, but there is no way I am showing up to his house in it with somebody else driving. I want to hear love and inspiration from him not hellfire and brimstone."

"Okay. Okay, you drive. I will head over now. See you."

"See you soon," she says and hangs up. Danielle panics a little. Oh my God, Chris is coming. What should I wear? She runs over to the closet and looks. She takes a brief gander at her mother's engagement dress, as she now calls it, but decides she wants Chris, and all the other nonfamily men in the room to concentrate on Grandpa Roberto and not her. Instead, she chooses a dress she wore to church back home. She puts a little makeup on, and goes outside to wait for Chris.

On their way over Danielle explains to Chris that in the meeting, people do something called speaking in tongues with interpretation. Chris tells her that he has heard of that stuff before, and that it would not bother him. Danielle is relieved and again very intrigued by this fascinating young man.

When they arrive, Nana is waiting outside for them. Danielle called ahead to let her know that Chris was coming as well. Nana practically runs up to the car and gives them both a big hug and kiss, and ushers them inside. Everybody is already there and seated when Chris and Danielle come in and sit down. Chris looks around and is pleasantly surprised at how much the scene before him reminds him of the big family get together at Thanksgiving his own family has every year.

The room is filled with people of all ages, from young children to older adults. He recognizes a lot of enlisted off-duty Coast Guard folks, even one or two from his own command at Brazos. He is glad to be off duty himself and not in uniform, so everything can be casual in the Chief's home. Nana leads the meeting and they do what she calls manifestations, which includes speaking in tongues with interpretation. The messages are something like Bible prophecy and prayer, but different. Chris thinks to himself, *if God inspired those messages, then He really does care about people.*

Roberto's teaching of the Scripture is magnificent. He has them all turn to the Book of Esther in the Old Testament and shows how Esther and her adopted father Mordecai prayed to God, worked together, and saved their people from total genocide. "Esther had to be very brave to do what she did," Roberto says as he finishes his presentation. "She was successful because she did not let fear stop her from doing what is right. She worked with her father to get the job done, and stand against all the evil that Haman brought against them. God bless you!" Roberto says as he closes the meeting.

Later that morning, Danielle and Chris are standing on the front porch with Nana eating some cookies and talking. Nana smiles at Chris and says, "I am glad you enjoyed our fellowship, Chris. You are welcome anytime."

"Thank you, Ma'am. I may take you up on that, especially now that I know Danielle comes. I can share a ride with one of the guys at Brazos."

"You know, Chris," says Nana, "this porch has a lot of Edwards and Garcia family history to it."

"Oh my God, Nana, you're such a schemer," Danielle says almost choking on a cookie.

Nana looks slyly at both of them and proceeds to tell the story about how she had used that dress Danielle wore the other night at the grand opening of Jacob's Ladder many years ago to push Jacob to propose to Danielle's mother. "He walked around with that darned ring in his pocket for almost a month after asking Roberto permission for Mary's hand. I just got tired of waiting, so I did what any good mother would do. I expedited the situation."

By the time Nana finishes with what is probably one of her favorite stories, Danielle and Chris are about as beet red as two human beings can get, and very awkwardly try to avoid eye contact with one another.

"Nana, Nana!" Chief Roberto exclaims as he joins the trio. "Quit embarrassing Danielle and Chris."

"Oh, Roberto. Danielle should know these things about her family. Besides, big tough guys like you, Jacob, and Chris here can sometimes be the biggest chickens when it comes to a beautiful woman. Or do I need tell them how long it took you to ask me to marry you? You old sea dog."

Roberto rolls his eyes and says, "Isabella Garcia, I believe one of your sons needs your help with his daughter over there, why don't you go see what's up?"

Nana laughs, gives her husband a big kiss, and heads off the porch to another granddaughter in need of her help.

"Sorry kids. Sometimes Nana can get a little pushy, but her heart is bigger than the state of Texas," Roberto says with both admiration and apology at the same time.

"That's okay, Chief. By the way, you are quite the orator. You really made that story about Esther seem real and alive."

Roberto puts his thumbs in the front part of his belt, throws his chest out and says, "Oh, it's a real story all right. When I was studying to put that presentation together, I couldn't help but think of Danielle and Jim." He looks at his granddaughter with pure love and compassion. "You two are like that. There is nothing you couldn't face down together. You just need the Lord's help to do it."

Danielle is stunned but also amazingly encouraged by her grandfather's words. "Grandpa Roberto, I would have to be a fool to not notice how strong and true your belief in God is. It has a very profound effect on my life and I think on Grandpa Jim's as well."

Danielle and Chris finally leave Roberto and Isabella's house, happy and excited about the quality experience they just had. Standing on the porch, Roberto watches his only grandchild from his late daughter Mary drive away with a fine young man who has just earned his approval.

Isabella steps up to her husband and puts herself under his loving arm. "You like this Lieutenant Rottanelli, I can see that. He is a fine young man."

Roberto smiles at the love of his life and says, "Yes, I like him. Our granddaughter is safer now that he is in her life. I have always known that an evil darkness has been after Jim and his family ever since Cozumel. But I have seen God's grace there too, and I think we are going to see an end to all this despair sooner than we might think."

"I pray that you are right, Roberto. I pray you are right," Isabella says as she lays her head on Roberto's strong and supporting shoulder.

Chapter Six

Big Business — Big Plans

Manheim, Three Weeks Later

Boris, annoyed with the archaic surroundings he has subjected himself to for almost a decade, sits in his office at the Edwards Auto complex. "What I'm building," he says to himself, "is worth it." No one would ever guess that the wholesale seller–client of Edwards Auto is also one of the world's most successful assassins, and wealthiest crime syndicate bosses alive. He continues to encourage himself, thinking, *my empire is vast and continues to grow. Soon all organized crime in the Americas will depend on me for their paychecks.* He picks up his phone and calls one of the few people alive that he even partially trusts. After the second ring, a female voice answers.

"Hello, Father."

"Hello, Natasha. We are about ready to implement the final stages of our plan."

Natasha's coquette is as developed as Barbara. Her prowess in deception and manipulation is almost as keen as her father's. "Do you want me to head to South Texas and make sure Yuri is staying up on all of his obligations and responsibilities, Father?"

Boris smiles with pleasure. "Yes, Natasha. I am also sending Alyeks from the Russian Ballet Academy there at the end of the week. You will act the part of his assistant. He will be there to make Danielle believe that he wants to recruit dancers from her school. You know how Alyeks feels about us, and you also know how we control him and his family. So keep him on a tight leash and make him very convincing to Danielle. Is my personal yacht on its way, and have you appropriated a suitable boat for our plan?"

Natasha loves being a step ahead of her father's expectations. "Of course, Father. All is prepared; and before you ask, I have already contacted our friends in Mexico. They will have a suitable and convincing group of pirates ready to do what they do so well to the people on that boat."

"Excellent, Natasha. This is going to be the final stage in a plan that has taken over twenty-five years to accomplish. My empire will be one of the biggest and most powerful in the world. Next to me, you have contributed the most to its success so far. Goodbye, Natasha, keep me updated on all points as we proceed."

"I will, Father. I will."

Natasha knew that was about as close to a compliment as she would ever get from her father. He personally took her on an important mission thirteen years ago when they had boarded that cruise ship in Miami. She made all the arrangements with the pirates, and for her father's personal yacht to be at the right place at the right time in Cozumel. It was she who used her father's influence to get the people in place on the barge and the tanker.

After the siege by the three boats was successful, her father's yacht showed up with the real professionals and found Barbara. The information she was able to steal from President Gonzalez's personal safe was key in having the Mexican Customs office under their influence. She met the boarding party and brought her father's one true love back to him, his Russian sniper rifle.

Only two things went wrong that day. First, the stupid pirates on that old cutter that she had upgraded with brand new turbo diesel engines panicked and opened fire with the Goon Guns that the Harrington's had gotten them when the Coast Guard cutter maneuvered past. And the second, her father failed to kill Commander Edwards with the sniper rifle.

That is when his obsession over Chief Roberto Garcia started. Natasha could not believe how obsessed her father was with that man. It was almost like he was afraid of him. He never let anyone try to take care of the menacing chief. As far as Boris was concerned, that was a complete no-fly zone for everyone. Even when the chief and his wife would visit the Edwards in Pennsylvania, Boris would always make sure he was out of town until the chief had left.

It was a real enigma to her because all the chief ever did was throw Jacob to the ground after the first shot that her father missed. After the third shot, his anger was the most violent she had ever seen in him, like a child's uncontrollable temper tantrum. He started screaming with rage, throwing and breaking things. It was almost like he thought it was Roberto's fault that he missed. Then, just as sudden as his outburst, he calmed down, grabbed his gun, located Barbara, and the three of them left and boarded the yacht before any of the others could join them.

She objected to the recruitment of that pig Jamaican who botched the job ten years earlier with the minister and his family off the coast of Honduras, when they obtained the documents that gave her father significant influence over the Mexican cartels. He failed to destroy the vessel. Her father insisted that the kind of terror the Jamaican could elicit in people would prove useful. The man could rape and kill with the theatrics of a Hollywood movie serial killer.

After Cozumel it seemed like things went sideways. She did, however, enjoy watching Commander Edwards fling the Jamaican pig off the cruise ship. It took her and her father ten more years to work up a good scenario where Jim and Jacob Edwards could be taken out. No one expected Danielle to go on that trip to Australia, but Boris blew a head gasket when Jim himself decided not to go. Danielle would have been easily manipulated to sell with her whole family wiped out, but Jim's survival set them back these past three years to work out another plan. It did not help when Danielle moved down to be with the chief and his family. Natasha did not see it for herself, but the reports she received about her father suggested that his tantrum to that was similar to the one on the cruise ship.

Putting all these thoughts out of her mind, she picks up her phone and dials a number. On the first ring, a sophisticated Russian voice answers the line. "Hello, Natasha."

"Alyeks, my friend. How is everything going? Are you ready for your trip to the United States?"

"I am ready. Will I be able to see my brother when we are there? It has been more than two years, and I want to know if he is really responding to the chemo like you have told me he is."

"You will be allowed to briefly visit him only after the mission is complete, and that is final."

Alyeks presses. "How do I know you even have him there? I have seen nothing and have only heard from you."

"Oh, Alyeks. Your lack of trust is hurtful. Should I let my father in on your lack of confidence in us?"

"No, please. I do not want him angry with me. I just want my family taken care of."

Natasha loves the fear that mention of her father inspires in people and hopes someday soon they will fear her like they fear him. "Alyeks, did we not get you that position at the academy because of your usefulness in the business in the Ukraine? Have we not kept your name from any responsibility to that little endeavor?"

"Yes, you have Natasha. But helping you develop a money laundering relationship with the Ukraine mafia is not something I am proud of, nor do I want it to be made public, especially now."

"Nor do we, but your associates down there would be very interested in the extra revenue you accumulated in that deal, would they not?"

"Yes, Natasha. I know, but I needed that money for my brother. The cancer was killing him. I had no choice."

"We understand that, Alyeks. That is why my benevolent father had him moved to a better facility in the United States where he could receive much better care."

Alyeks huffs. "Moved him first and then told me what he did is more like it. He kidnapped him to hold yet another weight over my head."

Natasha laughs and tells Alyeks that is the price he pays for knowing her father. "You do what he says or your family and loved ones will pay for your disobedience."

She tells him that they will meet in Houston and drive down together in a rented car to the yacht rental facility where they will board a luxury yacht and sail down to South Padre Island. Then they will meet her father and Yuri.

Done with that conversation, Natasha packs a few things for her trip to Padre Island where she will babysit Yuri through the final stages of the plan. After, she will drive up to Houston to meet Alyeks. She calls her cousin Yuri to inform him of her arrival later that day.

Yuri is not big on brains, and his lack of intelligence is further aggravated by his enormous ego. "Just never forget who the boss is, Natasha. All of Uncle Boris' holdings on this side of the world are in my name. That makes me his second-in-command. I will tolerate none of your usurping of my authority."

Natasha has a short fuse when it comes to Yuri, and he has a few scars to prove it. "The only authority you have, you little cockroach, is to do exactly what my father and I tell you to do. The only reason you have all my father's holdings in your name is because that sniveling coward who was your father took Boris' only sister and snuck away to the United States, then cursed the world by giving birth to you, thus making you an American citizen. You know that none of my father's holdings are in his name, but that does not stop him from controlling every iota of his empire. That includes you, you little worm. Remember your father, Yuri. Your compliance is the only thing that keeps you from his fate."

Yuri, sufficiently tamed by Natasha's tirade, promises to be there when she arrives and to do anything that her father tells them to do. Natasha has never been troubled with sentimentality concerning family, and that especially goes for her perverted little cousin Yuri. Once when she was only fifteen years old, Yuri thought that he would take advantage of his younger cousin while she was visiting from Russia. He still carries a rather nasty scar across his abdomen for that mistake. The memory gives her great pleasure as she leaves her penthouse apartment in Moscow to make her way to the airport for her flight to New York and then on to New Orleans where her father's yacht will be waiting. From there, she will sail to Corpus Christi where she is now sure Yuri will be nervously awaiting her arrival.

*   *   *

"Danielle Edwards, Nonprofit Dance Instruction, may I help you?"

"Danielle, this is Alyeks Yeshlton of the Russian Ballet Academy. I don't know if you remember me, but I saw you dance three years ago in Philadelphia at Temple University. We were introduced by a mutual friend."

"Alyeks! Yes, I do remember you very well. I am still not interested in a man twice my age, no matter how famous he thinks he is."

"Miss Edwards, although I do find you to be extraordinarily beautiful, the purpose of my call is purely professional. My academy is sending me on a recruiting itinerary to the United States to look for young and gifted dancers, especially young males. I am told that you have a sixteen-year-old Latino boy there who is an expert salsa dancer, trained by his mother who was a famous dancer from Mexico City years ago. I've heard that for the last two years he has shown incredible ability in ballet, is this true?"

Danielle takes a moment to process all this. How could someone like Alyeks Yeshlton even know about her little school all the way down in Texas? "Why, yes Alyeks. His name is Juan and he is one of the most vivacious raw talents I have ever met or worked with. How on earth did he ever get on your radar?"

Alyeks gulps inwardly knowing he has to play this just right or he will blow the whole thing. "Why, by another mutual friend who resides in Pennsylvania and works with your grandfather there, of course."

"You're not talking about Boris, are you?"

"Yes yes, Boris. His family has long been a benefactor of the Russian Ballet Academy and he is the one that alerted us to this young Juan you're working with."

"So, Boris has connections to the Russian Ballet Academy, huh? Is there anything that old guy doesn't dabble in?" Danielle asked, a bit perplexed.

Alyeks thinks to himself, *you have no idea, young woman. No idea at all.* "You see," Alyeks says as he refocuses, "Boris is coming down to south Texas to help his nephew, Yuri, finalize some sort of deal with the Mexican businesses that are buying his cars. He heard from Jim that you are to have a recital that same weekend. His contacts in the academy told him I would be in the Southwest United States during that time, so he insisted that I come down and enjoy your students' performance. Boris' family connections are such that the academy tries to indulge their request whenever they are made. I did some checking of my own and came across a newsreel from a local station down there showing bits of an earlier performance by this young dancer, Juan, and I have to admit that my curiosity is piqued about this one."

"Well, if Alyeks Yeshlton's curiosity is piqued about one of my little ole dancers, who am I to stand in the way? We will see you this weekend. I will have VIP tickets waiting for you when you arrive."

Alyeks was not kidding when he told Danielle he saw that clip of her dancers on the news. From what he could see, there was some amazing talent in that group and some professionally done choreography as well. The boy Juan was a potential superstar.

Danielle sat at her little desk in the dance studio, totally dumbfounded that Boris could turn out to be any kind of a benefactor, especially to her and her students. She finally decided that it had to be about business. She remembered how Grandpa had told her that Boris offered to buy out Edwards Auto more than once. She decides that she should keep her guard up this weekend just in case he tries to pull any leverage over her grandpa by using her or one of her students. She taps her phone, taps Grandpa Jim in her contact book, and the phone dials.

"Hello, Grandpa. I hope I did not catch you at the wrong time, I just have a quick question."

"Danielle, it's never a wrong time for you to call me. Besides, it's still just Monday morning. Things are only beginning to heat up around here. What's up?"

"Well I just got a very interesting phone call from Alyeks Yeshlton of the Russian Ballet Academy. He wants to come to the recital this weekend for possible recruitment of some of my students; Juan in particular. You remember Alyeks? He's the one who came to the fall recital at Temple in my senior year and started hitting on me. I thought for sure Daddy was going to kill him when he found out. Anyway, he is one of the most important dance instructors in the world. How does a Podunk, New York–based wholesaler like Boris have influence over him and a place as prestigious as the Russian Ballet Academy?"

Jim kind of rolls his eyes as he responds, "Geez, Danielle. I don't know. I believe he told me it's through family connections or something. Anyway, we are flying down there together. He has to check on Yuri and that whole import deal across Mexican border lines. That reminds me, could you meet Yuri over at the customs office and sign some paperwork for Edwards Auto and make sure it gets notarized? Barbara says I forgot to sign some of the papers and it got sent before she could catch it."

"Sure, Grandpa. Oh, and please tell Barbara to dress more conservatively at work. All those other dealers hang out there way too much just so they can flirt with her, and Tony told me that the guys are always trying to sneak up front to look at her."

Jim gives a hearty laugh. "You know she and I came to an understanding about that a few weeks ago. She has been very good about wearing business appropriate clothing while at work ever since. You wonder why I keep your name on the Board of Trustees for the business. Hell, honey, you still run the place from all the way down in Texas. Oh, please don't forget Yuri. That's over two hundred units. That is a lot of moolah to be hung up in customs, you know."

Danielle assures Jim that she will get Yuri's precious papers signed and notarized, tells him she loves him, and hangs up.

She walks out to the studio where Juan and the other dancers are waiting and gives them the exciting news about how the great Alyeks Yeshlton from the Russian Ballet Academy will be there this weekend for the recital. She finds it very refreshing that over half the kids have no clue who Alyeks is or why a Russian ballet school is any bigger of a deal than their own right here in South Texas. She does finally convince them, however, that having someone like Alyeks make a special trip just to come see them dance is a big deal and that they should really try to make Sunday's recital the best they have ever done.

Friday Afternoon

Boris walks into the main office of Edwards Auto to give Barbara her instructions for the final stages of his plans. Jim left a day early to go down to South Texas to be with Danielle and Roberto's family for the upcoming recital this weekend. He had put Tony and Barbara in charge of getting everything ready for the Friday sale, so

Barbara is at the computer registering cars at Manheim's Friday sale.

Boris stealthily approaches her from behind, unnoticed by the beautiful Honduras woman. As he puts his hands on her neck, he can feel the sudden fear pulse through his servant's body, which gives him an almost erotic pleasure. "I don't understand why you can't pick a more appealing outfit. You are supposed to be a distraction to men, always. That is your purpose in my organization."

She recovers herself and takes Boris' hands briskly off her neck. She spins around to face the animal that has enslaved her for more than half of her life. "Jim Edwards spurned my attempt at seduction and then offered me his continued support as his assistant with full access to all his business dealings. I have simply adapted, and am now playing that role so that I may still be of use in your plan to take over his business."

Boris, mildly surprised at the amount of defiance coming from this woman of late, drills his eyes into her soul and says, "Your Papa misses you. He does not get around as much as he used to and asks for you constantly. Your only way to fulfill his desire to see you depends on how useful you are to me. Have I not always made that quite clear, Barbara?"

Barbara, robbed once again of her momentary bravado, sits back down. She acknowledges that Boris' concerns are always of primary importance. He continues, "After this weekend, Yuri will be the owner of Edwards Auto, though it will take some time for the transition to be permanent. In the end, this place will be fully under my control and your services will no longer be needed in the United States. I have some concerns in South America that your specific skillset will accommodate very well. In other words, don't get too comfortable here. This is very temporary for you."

Boris tells her to prepare for his return on Monday and that turmoil will ensue as Yuri begins to assume ownership. She gives him his airplane ticket to Houston, Texas. He walks out of the main building with one more stop before he heads to the Harrisburg Airport. Boris walks around the corner and across the lot between the main building and their rented facility. He passes the two large, empty bays that will soon be the diesel mechanic shop, takes a left at the end of the building, and approaches a door that has an Edwards Auto Transport sign over it. Boris is quite fond of this section of Jim's business because it is this arm of Edwards Auto that really got him interested in controlling the business twenty years ago.

At first, he tried to make do with the company he started under Yuri in New York. He had five transport trucks there and he would use those to get his cars to Manheim. After they sold, he would truck them down to South Texas where they were unloaded at the custom yard and picked up by his people in Mexico. The cartels then took the shipments to their own holding yards, retrieved their cash from the units and disposed of the units, as they saw fit. What Boris did not like is that the same trucking line that brought the cars to Manheim were taking them out again. He thought this was too much of a coincidence for some intelligent FBI or NSA agent to ignore. So, having his clients hire Edwards Auto to transport the vehicles to South Texas was another layer of camouflage that suited his sensitive nature.

It annoyed Boris that he had to become such a savvy auto wholesaler over the years to keep up the masquerade. He couldn't have his clients bid stupid money for the cars he sold at the auction because that would bring unwanted attention from many directions. No, he had to learn the game, get good at it, and make it look like he lived and died for every penny these stupid cars brought. Yuri's little wholesale operation here in Manheim might turn a profit of two to three million dollars a year if they were sharp.

Jim's was considered one of the five biggest in the world. He did over ten million a year. Boris knew that he could sometimes get that much money hidden in one vehicle. He made fifteen percent off that amount. A load of ten cars going down to South Texas could stash a potential of one hundred million dollars, of which he would make fifteen million. Boris sent out four to five truckloads a week and looked forward to tripling that someday. He always knew that the only way to be truly profitable as a crime syndicate in the United States was to keep everything on a cash basis, but two problems always came up. Number one, if you spend more than ten thousand at a time, all kinds of electronic red flags go up in little government monitoring offices all over the country. Two, if you try to deposit large amounts of money in any kind of banking institution, the IRS and many other agencies will be all over you.

The money had to be legitimized or cleaned somehow, and that usually involved a very expensive process that could cost the client as much as sixty percent of the funds. But, if one could somehow get the cash out of the country and to its prospective owners, they could afford to charge much less than traditional money launderers and by sheer volume make more profit. Boris' main clients were Mexican and South American crime cartels, but his reputation was growing and others were reaching out to his organization.

All these thoughts put a very big smile on Boris' old and crinkled face as he reaches his destination and walks into the head office of Edwards Auto Transport to meet Bob Billings.

Fifteen years ago, Bob was a two-bit smuggler working out of North Jersey, using his rig to transport just about anything for a buck, when he ran into Boris' nephew Yuri, who enlisted him in the organization, put him on the payroll and then had him apply to the then new Edwards Auto Trucking company, part of Edwards Auto, in Manheim. It took him about ten years of doing honest trucking to get promoted to manager, but Boris made sure he was well compensated for his patience and diligence.

Now, Bob made sure that all of Boris' money smuggling went completely unnoticed to anyone. Bob knew that Boris was a cold-blooded killer and would not hesitate to remove his own head if he gave him any reason to do so. Therefore, he played very nicely by Boris' rules.

Boris smiles at the trucker and says, "Bob, the final stages of my plan are in place. By this time next week, Yuri will take legal action to assume control of Edwards Auto, and there will be no one left alive who can counter that claim."

Bob stands up, "That is great news boss. Everything is in order for the next shipment, and Ivan and the boys are taking the units to the auction as we speak. Once they are sold, my guys will be ready to collect the cars from inside the auction, load them, and be off tonight as usual."

"Please sit, your diligence and obedience does not go unnoticed, my friend. Soon, I will be able to make you a much more wealthy man without drawing undue attention to it."

"Works for me, boss," Bob says and then asks if Boris has anything else he wants him to do.

Boris considers the requests and tells Bob to start looking for ten more used tractor-trailer units for sale. He says it is about time they begin to double their shipments down south. He then brings up his concerns for Ivan and the sloppy way he has handled things lately.

"Boris, whatever changes you want to make around here, I am your man," Bob exclaims with his North Jersey cocky bravado.

"That is good to know, my friend. Loyalty is something that I value above most qualities in my associates, and so far, yours has been exemplary. For now, just keep an eye on him and Barbara, and report to me anything unusual. But now, I have a plane to catch and a family to extinguish. Goodbye, Bob."

Bob stands again as Boris leaves and stretches out his hand, but to his disappointment, it is not received by the other, so he just says, "Goodbye boss, let me know if you need anything else."

When Boris leaves, Bob plops down in his chair, reaches into his drawer and pulls out a bottle of vodka that Yuri gave him earlier that month. He takes a good long swig and wipes his mouth with the other hand. He thinks to himself, *how can that old bag of bones scare the hell out of me like that?* He brushes it off and goes outside to make sure everything is ready to roll for the next shipment. *Funny,* he thinks, *never in my life did I think I would be shipping hundreds of millions of dollars of anything. Here I am, actually shipping that much dough every week.*

Chapter Seven

Signs, Wonders, and Moving Mountains

Saturday Morning, Around 1 a.m.

The storm hits the Delaware Bay like a thunderbolt. A few spectators, clinging to the rail out on the dock, hair blowing wildly, see the most bizarre thing they have ever witnessed happen right before their eyes.

To some, it's as if the Greek gods Zeus and Poseidon are at war, and Zeus throws a lightning bolt of power into the middle of the bay and causes a whirlwind of commotion in the sea. A gigantic black rectangular box lurches up out of the bay, surges toward the shore, crashes into a large bar and grill sign hanging over the edge of the shore walk, and then starts to spin and skip up the Delaware River like a pebble skipping across a pond.

In awe, they watch it skip out of sight.

Saturday Morning, Philadelphia Office of the FBI

Deputy Director Chuck Yeager sits at his desk, staring at an old picture of him and his Kings Point roommate, Jacob Edwards, on their graduation day. It was the same day that both of them were commissioned into the United States Coast Guard. They spent their first seven years serving together in the Caribbean. He still couldn't accept the fact that Jacob died over three years ago in that plane wreck.

It was so fantastic when the both of them had lived so close to each other. They were back to being best friends all over again, going on fishing and hunting trips, and taking their families to the shore. Jacob's dad, Jim, had a pretty nice beach house in Ocean City, Maryland, and sometimes, if they could work it out, they would spend a whole week down there with their families. When Danielle went to Temple University, there was hardly a week where she was not over at his house having dinner or just hanging out. Chuck got married and started having children about ten years after Jacob did, so his three were all in junior high and high school now. Danielle proved to be a wonderful babysitter for his children and friend to his wife, Martha.

When they heard about the plane crash over the Pacific, he and Martha called Danielle who was already on her way to Manheim to be with Jim. Concerned for her safety, Chuck and Martha left their children with friends and drove to Manheim to offer whatever help they could. He just could not stomach that Jacob, Mary, and Linda were dead. It seemed so wrong. He had stopped looking into the Cozumel incident a few years back, much to the relief of Jacob Edwards. But after the crash, his gut kept telling him that it was somehow all connected.

For three years now, he was quietly looking into the whole thing all over again. The clincher was the Russian and his girlfriend who got away with the nanny on the speed yacht. Though most of the photos from the cruise line were clear enough to show a blond-haired man in his middle to late fifties accompanied by a very attractive brunette in her early twenties, they could not get a facial recognition on either of them from any data base around the world. But Chuck had always been sure about two things. One, that the Russian's target was Jacob, and two, that the high-powered Russian rifle was brought on board by the pirates who came from the modified luxury yacht.

Chuck had done some pretty extensive research on the rifle to see if any known assassinations had been linked to it. He did find a series of hits, mainly in Europe and South America where the SV-98 Russian sniper rifle was used. The hits were all linked to an assassin that people just called "The Chameleon" because he would first take on a persona that fit in with the culture of his victims, study them for a while hiding in plain sight, and then he would plan out his perfect kills. Most were crime syndicate related, but a few were political. The curious thing is that the reports start in 1969 and stop in 1988.

After the last date, it appears that this very successful assassin retired. Not really a surprise, considering that after almost twenty-some years, with something in the neighborhood of fifty hits, whoever this guy was or is, he would have been a very wealthy man by 1988.

The question that gnawed at Chuck is why did the assassin suddenly resurface sixteen years later to try to kill a captain of a Coast Guard *Hamilton-class* cutter? Chuck could not find anything that would connect Jacobs' dad to a crime syndicate. Although Edwards Auto was a respectable wholesale operation in Manheim, it wasn't some multibillion-dollar high profile corporation that could justify a world class assassin like this guy.

With these thoughts churning in his mind, Chuck gets up, looks out the window, and admires this old city of brotherly love he's been assigned to all these years.

Being only the last weekend in August, it was a little early for hurricane season, which usually brought heavy storms, but last night was a doozie. All the boats along the Delaware River were hunkered down all night and weathered through. Chuck had not heard of any severe property damage or deaths related to the storm yet, but all emergency agencies—including his own—were on standby and ready if needed.

Just then, his office intercom chirps and one of the agents says, "Chuck, we just got a call from Philly PD, seems they found a cargo container with a reported stolen 2013 Toyota Camry and the body of a dead white male, mid-forties. Deceased at least two to three weeks."

Chuck presses the intercom button to respond. "Okay, what does that have to do with us? Can't the PPD handle?"

"Yes, Chuck. They could, but the container belongs to the Mancini family, and the Camry was reported missing by the father of your friend, Jacob Edwards."

"Okay, so there's a lot of coincidence. But why call the FBI?"

"Well," says the agent, "the PPD officer in charge says you tried to investigate the owner of the Camry a few years ago—a Russian named Yuri, and his uncle Boris, out of New York City. He says neither of you got anywhere trying to figure out who this Boris is or where in Russia he came from."

Light bulbs go off in Chuck's head. A "Russian James Bond," was what Jacob said. Chuck remembers the first time he had seen Boris; early sixties then, must be pushing seventy by now. He met him right outside Jacob's office, caught on right away that Jacob did not think much of the guy. That is why he decided to investigate him, but nothing turned up. Hell, he never even saw the guy again. He really wasn't what you would term a major player, even in the auto auction business. Just some glorified salesman in his nephew Yuri's company. Whenever he would go to Manheim to visit the Edwards, Boris would never be around the business. It was like he never wanted to run into Chuck at all.

Oh my God! How could I be so stupid? Thunderbolts of lightning begin to flash in Chuck's head. He opens the door into the borough's main lobby and tells his assistant to get his top crime investigation people to that dock stat and start going over every square inch of that cargo container. He grabs his gear and out the door he goes.

Down at the dock, Chuck stands musing in front of the opened Mancini container. "So you're telling me that this container was dropped into Delaware Bay, it suddenly resurfaced, and the storm blew the container back up the river until it was seen this morning just bobbing off the dock here?" Chuck asked the Philadelphia police detective and the FBI crime scene investigation unit team leader.

"Director Yeager, I know it sounds ridiculous but that is exactly what the evidence we've been able to piece together tells us so far."

Chuck is writing furiously in his notebook. "That's almost seventy miles upriver. How can you possibly determine that it was dropped off in Delaware Bay in the first place?"

"Well for starters, Chuck, we found this stuck to the locking lever bar of the door hinge." The Philly police detective hands him a piece of a sign that reads, *Cape May Fish-N-Chips*, then continues, "It was reported broken off last night in the storm by a big black cargo container flying out of the water, confirmed by at least three witnesses."

He tells Chuck about how unique that damn storm was. Basically, it followed the same path as the container and then dissipated earlier that morning. Chuck was about to hit fifteen years with the FBI and he had seen a lot of weird stuff in those years, but a storm bringing him a piece of evidence that could break open one of the biggest mysteries the borough has ever had was brand new to him.

"Well then, what is this container telling you so far?" Chuck asks, folding his arms.

The FBI crime scene unit affirms that the cargo container belongs to the Mancini family shipyards and that it was shown as shipped out over three weeks ago. It was reported lost in a storm in the Indian Ocean about a week later. But they confirm that it blew up from Delaware Bay because all the chemical tests done and residue on the outside indicates that it has not been anywhere else. They show Chuck how holes were drilled into the container to probably let the water fill in, but that a plastic tarp inside the container got caught in the holes and prevented the air from leaking out, which made for a much more buoyant container that the wind and water could catch in the storm and move more easily.

They note that the Toyota Camry is registered to a Yuri Sebastion who has a wholesale operation in Manheim and a small trucking business in Queens, New York.

"And get this," one of the investigator's says, "he is a full partner with a former Coast Guard Admiral in one of the largest banking conglomerates on the East Coast; Harrington Enterprises."

Chuck can't believe it. He is talking about the man who was the vice commandant when he served. "James Harrington?" he says, "I know that old blueblood windbag. He wouldn't partner with some little Russian car salesman unless you held a gun to his head. This just gets weirder and weirder. What about the dead body?"

"That would be one Alan Rogers, an independent paintless dent removal guy who worked in Manheim."

Chuck remembers meeting him at Jim and Jacob's place a couple of times; a nice guy but definitely more concerned about making money than anything else. He asks if the body has told them anything. They tell Chuck that Alan's throat was cut open by some sharp wire and that he quickly bled to death. On his stomach, written in his own blood, is the name Ivan.

"How in the world could a man who died so quickly write that on his stomach in the presence of the murderer?" Chuck shakes his head, totally perplexed.

They assure him that they have no idea but that's exactly what they found. They say that there is one Ivan Sorenzo who works for Yuri as the shop foreman at his wholesale detail shop at the Edwards complex in Manheim.

Chuck looks at the detective with wide eyes.

"Yes, Chuck," the detective interjects, "I have a unit on its way to pick up Ivan for questioning right now."

Chuck is well aware of Ivan and Yuri, and it bothers him because he knows they are both morons by anyone's standards. He could definitely see Ivan killing someone and probably being stupid enough to write his name on him, but he sincerely doubts that Yuri can brush his own teeth without help. "This is not adding up at all. Everything looks too thought through, too professional for those imbeciles."

Chuck opens his hands and spreads his arms out in an appealing gesture as he states, "Let's all agree that it is a pure miracle that we even have this container to look at. By all the laws of physics, this thing should be at the bottom of the bay full of water, never to be seen again. Ivan and Yuri are two lowlife idiots who don't have half the brains between them to be doing anything with banking, professional murder or evidence disposal like this. Someone else is calling the shots and pulling the strings here and I may have a hunch who."

He stares off for a second thinking. "Hey, are you familiar with the recent Mancini hit case at all?"

"Yes, I am," one of the investigators answers.

"Did they figure out what kind of rifle was used?"

"Well, yeah, they did. Get this, they said it was a slug from a Russian SV-98."

Chuck stares off, stunned. How could he have missed it for so long? After a brief pause, he nods and says, "If I'm right, this may end up being one of the biggest cases of the twenty-first century." Chuck turns to leave and the Philly Police detective grabs his arm.

"Chuck, what's up here?"

"Just hold on, Holmes," he says, "I have to be sure about this before I shoot my mouth off. I need to go check on a Russian James Bond that I have been hunting for a very long time."

He walks away from the detective, gets in his car and heads toward Manheim where he believes he will catch the man who killed his best friend, his friend's wife and mother—and who has probably been trying to kill Jacob's whole family for over fourteen years now.

*　　*　　*

Barbara sits in Jim's office, thinking about Boris driving away in that ridiculous Hummer of his yesterday. She never thought she would stand up to him like she had, and that she'd do it twice. Granted, brief at best, but she still stood up to her master for all practical purposes, and she lived. All she can think is that something in her changed that day it became clear that Jim Edwards would never succumb to her charms. She should have been insulted, but instead she felt liberated by the jovial honesty and the sincere care he showed for her as a person. *My God,* she thought, *if any man ever loved me the way Jim loved his deceased wife, I would think I was in heaven for real.*

She realizes she has served the man who killed Jim's family and has been instrumental in all the deceit and manipulation of his family for so long. It pierces her heart to think about it. Boris treats her like a dog. She hates it. If only she could change it all. All that remorse, all the death, the hell she lives in now.

That's it, it's too much. She makes up her mind, *not anymore.*

She's going to make up for the wrongs she's caused, and try to save what is left of this wonderful and almost wiped-out family. No matter what, no matter the threat to her own life, or Papa's, she has to do this.

She knows exactly who to reach out to—someone from another family that she hurt so long ago.

She reaches inside a secret place in her purse and pulls out a piece of paper with a phone number belonging to a Mexican Naval Task Force captain who she has not seen since her eighteenth birthday. She takes a deep breath and types the number into the company phone on Jim's desk.

The phone rings twice and a hard female voice answers, "*Fuerza de Tarea contra el Cartel.*"

Barbara takes a deep breath. "Captain Marnia Gonzalez, please."

"Barbara?!" An astonished voice answers.

After acknowledging who she is and noting she has a lot to say, she spends the next two hours explaining every detail of her life to Marnia starting from that horrible day on the finance minister's yacht with the brutal murder of his family, and the torture and rape of his thirteen-year-old daughter at the hands of the same Jamaican who brutalized Marnia years later. She explains how Boris hid her father from her and uses him to coerce her to do his bidding. How he took her to South America and had her trained in the art of seduction at high-priced brothels; then had her educated at a college in Russia in business and finance so that she could gain employment with people who he wanted to seduce and manipulate.

She was allowed to see her father only once a year on Boris' yacht, usually in a port on a South American dock in the winter time.

It was really hard for Barbara to admit to Marnia that her affair with her father was to manipulate him so that she would gain access to his dealings with the cartels in Mexico, and his influence over the customs going across the border from Texas to Mexico. The worst was when she had to explain the whole incident at Cozumel and the cruise ship birthday party.

"I had all the documents that Boris needed to move ahead with his plans. Normally he would have extracted me out of Mexico City, but he saw an opportunity with your upcoming birthday party. He needed to control a legitimate United States trucking company associated with the Manheim Auto Auction in Pennsylvania for his money laundering smuggling operation. He set his eyes on Edwards Auto to meet his need."

She explained that in Boris' opinion, the best way to take over that company would be to eliminate the heirs; the most prominent one was Jacob Edwards, then Commander of the United States Coast Guard *Hamilton-class* cutter, *First Responder*. He was responsible for patrolling that area of the Gulf at the time.

"Barbara, are you telling me that the whole Cozumel scenario happened to lure the man who saved my life, a great hero to the Mexican people, to his death?"

Barbara sighs, "That is exactly what I am telling you. Boris knew that once the Coast Guard cutter positioned itself between the pirate cannon and the cruise ship, he would have a clear shot at Commander Edwards on the command deck."

Barbara goes on to say how no one expected the pirates on the ship to attack the Coast Guard thus exposing the cannon as a fake, which caused the Coast Guard to retaliate with their own weapon. Boris had to take the shot prematurely, which he would have made on the second or third round if Chief Garcia had not thrown his son-in-law to the deck at exactly the right time. And that was the big game changer, because Boris knew that as soon as anyone attacked the Coast Guard, the United States Navy could intervene and if he waited too long there would be no escape for him. He had to get his accomplice and me out of there as soon as possible or all his carefully laid out plans would fail.

Barbara begins sobbing and chokes out through the gasps, "Marnia, I'm so sorry that I left you alone with that animal Jamaican. It all happened so fast. First he killed those three bodyguards, then he and his cronies held us at gunpoint as he picked one girl at a time to take them back to the kitchen to maul and rape. Two of your friends died that day, and the one that lived was never the same again." Marnia shudders as Barbara finishes the story. "Then Boris, disguised as a tourist, storms into the room with his daughter, tells me to get the package and come with him." Barbara, still sobbing, apologizes again for leaving Marnia there.

Marnia, astonished, reacts with deep compassion as she exclaims, "Barbara you did not leave me there. They almost killed you when you refused to leave. That pig

Boris backhanded you across the jaw, and the sleaze he was with put you in a choke hold and threatened to kill me if you did not go with them. You had no choice and I have never blamed you for anything but saving my life."

Barbara continues the story by telling Marnia how they fled to Boris' yacht, which was equipped with military grade armaments, stealth technologies, and high-powered engines that are not even available on the market. They left everyone—even the Jamaican—behind, and were able to reach one of Boris' secret ports in Central America before anyone could track them.

Marnia sits at her desk, asking key questions and furiously taking notes as Barbara illustrates every phase of Boris' operation that she is privy to, including the fact that Boris's daughter, is now the number two person in his whole operation.

As they both go over every detail of Boris' operation, two big black SUV's and three Police cars pull up to Edwards Auto's front lot. Three police officers and two men dressed in suits with assault gear that reads "FBI" head over to Boris' rented shop and enter. Seconds later, Ivan runs out of the front and dashes toward the employee parking lot but is tackled by the police and put into cuffs.

While she watches this unfold, a blond-haired man in his early fifties comes into the main office of Edwards Auto and introduces himself as Chuck Yeager, Deputy Director of the Philadelphia office of the FBI.

Barbara, in total shock and unable to think or speak, stares incredulously at the man. Barely able to do anything else, she casts her eyes down and hands her phone over to Chuck.

He takes the phone from the astonished woman behind the desk who mumbles to him that the person on the phone can answer all of his questions.

"This is Chuck Yeager, Deputy Director of the Philadelphia FBI office. May I ask who I am speaking to?"

"Deputy Director Yeager, what a delightful surprise. I imagine you are there to apprehend Ivan; that's good. I suggest that you find and detain the trucking manager Bob Billings also. He is either out in the yard or over at the auto auction preparing to load and transport some automobiles that I am sure the FBI will find extremely interesting once you have examined them closely."

Chuck recognizes the Spanish accent, but also hears something familiar in this woman's voice. "Who are you and how do you know these things?"

"Director Yeager, we have met before. I am Captain Marnia Gonzalez of the Mexican Federal Police 3rd Military Brigade, Anti-Cartel Task Force."

It dawns on him; this is the same girl Jacob saved from that piece-of-shit Jamaican all those years ago. Her father was the Mexican president, and he's aware that she is now a rather passionate law enforcement figure called "The Cartel Crusher" in some circles.

"Marnia, we met at the funeral. How on earth did you get involved in this investigation?"

As the other law enforcement personnel roundup Bob Billings and question other employees of Edwards Auto and Yuri's shop, Chuck and Marnia thoroughly brief each other on this case that has rather miraculously landed in both of their laps today. Barbara sits back and waits her turn. She knows she will have a lot to answer for. But now that everything is coming out, she can't help but experience sensations that have not been a part of her life for decades—peace, safety, and joy.

Deputy Director Chuck Yeager of the FBI and Captain Marnia Gonzalez of the Mexican Federal Police quickly obtain authorization to form a joint task force to investigate the money laundering operation they have just discovered. Chuck agrees with Marnia that the only person they can pin this whole thing on is Yuri Sebastion, and they both know that he is simply a front man, but that his mysterious uncle, Boris, is the real culprit, which Barbara has confirmed. But they are going to need a lot more than the testimony of one woman, who dropped off the grid thirteen years ago, saying that he is the main guy. They need to catch him red-handed or get some hard evidence. They know that he is in South Texas and that he has a plot to somehow eliminate Jim and Danielle Edwards and gain control of their company at the same time. They need to act quickly.

Saturday, South Texas

Danielle did not like the idea of meeting Yuri alone, but the only person available to go with her was Juan. With Grandpa Roberto's encouragement, she took him along. Yuri told her that the only notary available at the time was in the marriage license office and he had to get the documents to the customs borough of Brownsville as soon as possible. Danielle felt uncomfortable being with a minor, but she also thought she could handle Yuri and his overactive hormones. It surprises her immensely when she walks in and sees Yuri with another woman; a dark-haired foreign woman, very beautiful, but familiar, in a subtle way.

Yuri walks up to Danielle, enamored with his own boyish bravada and thanks her for coming so early. "Danielle, I am so sorry for my drunken display at your grandfather's grand opening."

Danielle is somewhat flabbergasted at Yuri's openness, but accepts it as him trying to impress this foreign girl.

To everyone's surprise, the new girl walks up and extends her hand to Danielle. "Danielle Edwards, it is such a pleasure to meet you at last. I am Natasha, Alyeks Yeshlton's assistant here in the United States for his recruitment tour."

Danielle is a little taken aback, but it only heightens her suspicion that this whole deal is some kind of con for Boris to buy Grandpa Jim's company. Danielle decides that the direct approach is best. "Look guys, I know that Yuri's Uncle Boris wants Edwards Auto and thinks that by impressing me with a visit from the great Alyeks Yeshlton, he is going soften me to his way of thinking. My dancers are ecstatic about the whole thing, but you guys need to realize Grandpa cannot even sell Edwards Auto without my signature, as evidenced by me needing to sign these papers. It is a family business and I will never betray my father's memory or his trust. As long as I live, Edwards Auto is simply never going to be for sale!"

Natasha puts on her most innocent face. "My dear Danielle, I do not even know this Boris you speak of, but I can assure you that my only interest is in assisting Alyeks Yeshlton in finding outstanding new dancers for the renowned Russian Ballet Academy. That is why I am here. Your associate Yuri, whom I have just met, picked me up at the airport an hour ago and has procured a car for me to pick up Alyeks in Houston this afternoon."

Danielle, exasperated, gasps at Yuri and says, "Let's just get these papers notarized so Edwards Auto can release the cars to the Mexican transporters and I can get to my dancers to prepare them for Alyeks' historic visit to South Texas."

Yuri directs everyone to the marriage office where he approaches the window and shows the man behind the glass the paperwork he needs notarized. Danielle anxiously grabs the paperwork, signs the papers, and hands them to Yuri, who signs them as well. The man behind the desk notarizes the paperwork and hands it back to Yuri.

Danielle glares at him impatiently. "Just give me my copy so I can leave."

"I don't have copies right now, Danielle. I'm sorry; I'll have them for you tomorrow."

Danielle grabs the paperwork, walks over to the copy machine, puts a couple of quarters into the machine and makes her own copies. She gives the originals back to Yuri and storms out of the building with Juan in tow.

Natasha grabs the paperwork and backhands Yuri across his face, "You are the most spineless coward I have ever known. If anyone with expertise examines those copies, we are both very screwed and my father will probably execute us."

Yuri finds some testosterone deep inside and grabs Natasha with both hands by her throat. "Listen to me, you fucking whore. If you ever strike me again, I will kill you. After tomorrow, nothing that Danielle Edwards proposes will have any possibility of coming to pass because she'll be dead."

Natasha throws Yuri's hands off her and kicks him in the groin with obvious pleasure. Yuri falls to the floor in extreme pain as Natasha bends down and whispers alluringly in his ear. "The only one who may die at this point is you, you little worm. Make sure that the man behind the desk here can be counted on for his discretion in all matters that have transpired here."

Yuri takes a few minutes to get himself together and hobbles to the clerk's window. He reaches into his deep leg pockets and pulls out ten thousand more dollars in cash, and hands it to the marriage clerk with the promise of much more to come if he keeps his silence about all things that just happened. The man gulps and assures Yuri and Natasha that he can be counted on as he shoves the extra money into his pockets.

Yuri and Natasha walk out of the building to Yuri's car where Natasha takes out the paperwork and carefully peels back the cover of the front page to reveal a now notarized marriage license issued by the State of Texas to Danielle Edwards and Yuri Sebastion. The only thing it is lacking is the signature of a certified licensed Texas minister.

Natasha's cell phone rings. She looks but she already knows it is her father. "Hello Father, you will be pleased to know that we have the marriage license and are ready to proceed."

"Natasha, I truly believe that you are one of the very few human beings living who can truly serve my purposes. Most of the time I have to kill someone to get them to do what I want."

"Oh, Father. The mere threat of death often suffices to bend those we need to our will. Yuri is compliant. Barbara is compliant, and yes through death, Danielle and Jim Edwards will join the rest of their family and by that be compliant."

Boris is seated in a booth of a restaurant on Falcon Lake, Texas, ready to depart to Padre Island to meet up with everyone later that afternoon at that ridiculous fiasco of a restaurant, Jacob's Ladder. Though always pleased with his daughter's performance, Boris does not allow something as foolish as family sentimentality to distract him from his true source of power. He has built an empire by dealing out death in the right way, and at the right time. He vows to never let anything come between him and that power of death that has been so good to him.

He strokes the case that holds his unassembled high-powered rifle, then responds to his daughter with orders. "Go to Houston and pick up Alyeks from the airport.

Then go to the docks and join the luxury yacht we have rented for the occasion and take it down to Station Brazos. There we will meet. Yuri will pick me up and we will drive from Falcon Lake where we will meet up with Danielle, Jim Edwards, and some of Danielle's dancers at Brazos. The minister will be one of the guests on the yacht.

"We have to do this just right, Natasha. It all depends on Jim Edwards signing that contract, making Yuri the president of Edwards Auto. He will sign when confronted with the consequences. Have our friends in Mexico been notified of our rendezvous point?"

"Yes, Father. They will be in place at the appropriate time and will be awaiting your signal to proceed. What about Chief Roberto and his wife? Are you still concerned about them being there?"

Boris grinds his teeth and responds, "That Bible-thumping maggot has disrupted my plans for the last time. He and half his family will meet their compliance to my will at the emergency room in the Starr County Memorial Hospital later today. All is arranged."

Natasha is ecstatic at her father's foresighted wisdom. "You are truly the greatest artist of your craft, Father. We will see you soon."

"I know, Natasha. I know." Boris ends the connection, and looks at the Mexican man across from him in the booth.

"Make sure that the Doctor in the maternity wing of the hospital gets this package after you kill the Garcia family. Assist him in escaping if need be. If he causes any problems, kill him and return this package to Maximillian."

The man takes one look at the package and its contents, looks at the man sitting across from him and replies, "It will be done exactly as you say. My boss told me to follow your instructions to the letter, and I always do what he says."

Boris dismisses Maximillian's bush-league assassin, somewhat satisfied that he can handle the job given to him, and knowing that if he fails, he will discover how a true assassin operates. Boris sits back and waits for his dimwitted nephew, preparing himself to implement the final sequence of a plan that has been over fourteen years in the making.

Back at Padre Island

Danielle is glad to get that signing stuff out of the way. Dealing with people like Yuri and Boris is a part of the business she doesn't miss. Juan sits in the passenger seat with a blank stare as they head to Jacob's Ladder to meet up with the rest of the cast and wait for the bus to take them to Brazos and Alyeks' boat. Danielle looks at Juan and excitedly asks, "When is your father going to have the engine reinstalled in the Mustang, Juan?"

"Sometime today. All the upholstery is ready too. I can't wait to see what that car is going to look like all put back together. That chassis looks brand new now that the body shop is done."

Danielle starts to feel the old excitement about a project almost being completed. "Yup. I told you we could get all those genuine Ford parts if we were just patient, didn't I?"

"Yes, *Maestra*, you did." Danielle loved it when her students called her that. Grandpa Roberto told her once that it showed the very deepest of respect that her Spanish students had for her, and that she should never take it for granted.

As she pulls up to Jacob's Ladder, her cell phone rings. It's her grandmother Isabella. "Hi Nana what's up?"

"Oh Danielle, I am so sorry but Roberto and I have an emergency and we have to go to Starr County Memorial Hospital. Your Aunt Carmen is going in for an emergency c-section today and your uncle Willito is still out on patrol on Falcon Lake and cannot get back for a few more hours. We will definitely miss the cruise with Alyeks, and we still do not know if we can make it to the recital tomorrow."

Danielle sighs, but totally understands. She tells her nana to please keep her informed and that she will be praying for Uncle Willito and Aunt Carmen.

Isabella ends the phone call with Danielle with a thank you and a God bless. Roberto is driving. She can tell that he is deeply disturbed by this whole thing. She tells him that Danielle is fine with everything and is praying for her aunt and uncle.

Roberto gives a deep sigh and looks over at his wife. "Isabella, there is something very wrong about all of this. I feel like my whole family is in grave danger. I cannot put my finger on it yet, but the pressure I am feeling is as real as the air that we breathe."

Isabella takes a long look at her husband, grabs his right hand, closes her eyes, and prays with all her might. "God, You are all-knowing and all-caring. There is nothing too hard for You. You say in Your Holy Word that he who trusts in You will not be disappointed in his expectations. We lift our Willito and Carmen to You and thank You for their safety and that of our unborn grandchild. We also claim our granddaughter Danielle and Jim Edwards, her other grandfather. We claim their safety and Your guiding hand in their lives right now. Work mightily in us now that we can fulfill Your will in these situations, and back off the enemy with Your light and Your power. We give these concerns to You in Your wonderful son's name, our lord and our savior, Jesus Christ."

"Amen," says Roberto as he pulls Isabella's hand to his lips and tenderly kisses it. Roberto is renewed in his strength and trust in God to handle anything that is to come his way now. He thinks to himself, *with this woman at my side and the God that we both love and serve, mountains are going to have to move.*

CHAPTER EIGHT
EXTREME MEASURES —
EXTRAORDINARY THINGS

Starr County Memorial Hospital

Dr. Michael Kennedy could not believe how drastically his luck had changed in the last month. He thought for sure that the Mexican casino owner was going to kill him when he bet more than he had at the poker table and lost. Then, the mysterious Boris shows up out of nowhere, offers to pay off the whole debt—twenty-five thousand dollars—and promised him an additional hundred thousand if he would make sure that Carmen Garcia, her husband, and his parents were at the Starr County Memorial Hospital on this date by 7 p.m. He wanted them to miss a boat cruise he was hosting, that's all.

Two weeks ago, he added some medication that would subtly make her have abdominal pain in increasing frequencies, and he scheduled the last ultrasound for today at 2 p.m. Of course, when Carmen showed up, the first thing she complained about was her stomach pain, which made it very easy to then use the ultrasound to convince her that the baby was starting to go into breach and that he would have to do an emergency c-section that night to save her and the baby.

What he did not count on was her husband Willito being out on patrol until 7 p.m. but he could still work with that. The only other requirement was that Willito's parents, Roberto and Isabella Garcia, were also there. Dr. Kennedy was so relieved at not being killed that night and getting enough money to pay off a good deal of his student loans. And all Boris wanted was for them to miss a yacht party. Besides, Boris had said that if he could professionally pull off this little stunt, he would have much more lucrative work for him in the future. Michael Kennedy was always into making big money. That was why he became an OB-GYN in the first place.

He steps back into the examining room where the nurses are prepping Carmen for anesthesia. "Carmen, have you been able to reach Willito's parents? You said they are the closest relatives and I think it is very important that you have as much family around as possible."

"Yes, Dr. Kennedy. They will be here in an hour and so will Willito." Michael gives a palpable sigh of relief and tells her that he will wait for their arrival before he proceeds with the c-section.

Roberto and Isabella arrive at the hospital a little before 7 p.m. The first thing Roberto notices is all the Texas Rangers on the premises. With two sons who are sheriff deputies on Padre Island and one son in the Texas special highway patrol boat task force patrolling Falcon Lake, Roberto was very comfortable with law enforcement officers, and was well known in the South Texas circles. Roberto walks up to the man he recognizes as the Texas Ranger Major of the area and puts a hand on the big man's shoulder.

"John Brown, they have you working late today. What's the scoop?"

Major John Brown of Area D loves the Garcia family. They're just good people and Roberto is the patriarch of the whole clan. "Roberto! By God, I hear Carmen is here; I hope everything's all right. We are here on a high-profile cartel witness protection detail. They tried to assassinate him a couple weeks ago, and he just got cleared for some surgery, so we brought him here. The trial is in three weeks. He is our best bet at cracking down on a lot of drug smuggling and putting some pretty bad people away. I thought I'd better see this one through personally, so here I am."

Roberto pats his old friend on the back. "I've never known John Brown to not do the heavy lifting himself, even if his wife Susan will crack him over the head with a pot when he gets home for doing it."

"You got that right, *amigo*. I'll be sleeping outside with the dogs tonight."

Isabella reaches out and gives Major Brown a hug. "John, you know us girls always have to come first. Just show up with a dozen roses and a bottle of wine and she'll be okay."

John thanks Isabella for the advice and tells them both that due to the need for high security, the witness is being operated on in the emergency room. At Starr County Memorial Hospital, this is right next to the maternity wing where Carmen is. They both head over to see their daughter-in-law, and wait for their son to arrive.

A Chevy minivan and a Chrysler minivan pull up three blocks away from the hospital. They park in Lino's Pharmacy's parking lot in-between Pharmacy Road and Hospital Drive on State Rt. 3167. Pedro Lemacho, hit man for the Manerez Cartel, knows Major John Brown is no kindergartner when it comes to logistics. Starr County is an ideal location to move a high-profile witness like their target. There's only one circle drive leading into the premises and there's no real access from behind because it is all open ground. If he is going to pull this off, it's going to be tricky.

Pedro walks over to the other van and goes over the plan one more time with his team. The second van has a man and woman pretending to take their sixteen-year-old son to the emergency room to get treated for a dog attack. Just an hour earlier, Pedro and two others held the boy down as they stuck his bare leg through a hole cut in the kennel of a half-starved pit bull that they use for dog fighting across the border. The boy is half in shock, but the one thousand U.S. dollars he received made it well worth it to him.

They had decided to only carry small handguns with extra clips for easy concealment. They knew there were at least six Rangers at the hospital guarding the witness scheduled for surgery at 7 p.m. and that it would take ten to twelve minutes of response time for any reinforcements to arrive when called in. Pedro explains that everyone is going to drive over in their van, make the hits, dump their vans on the highway, and meet at his van in the pharmacy parking lot to get away.

The driver of the other van says it is a good plan, but asks why they have to go over to the maternity wing and hit this other family, the Garcias?

Pedro puts a very threatening hand on his comrade's shoulder. "Maximillian decides who lives and who dies. He wants that family just as dead as the pig *cavarone* traitor we are killing in the emergency room." He also adds, a bit more compassionately, "I have never known Maximillian to fear anyone, but this man Boris scares him, and that scares me. Plus, Boris paid one million dollars for this hit, so we are doing it. *Comprende?*"

"Yes, Pedro. I understand."

Pedro's with another woman and a younger man who could pass as his son. They get into the second van and drive over to the hospital emergency room.

Roberto cannot shake the feeling of wrongness about this whole day. He leaves his wife and daughter-in-law in the maternity ward and walks over to the parking lot to wait for his son to show up.

Just as he is rounding the corner, he sees a Chevy minivan pull into the emergency room offload area. Two couples and two boys —one who looks seriously injured —start to get out.

As the two men bend down to pick up the injured boy, Roberto can't believe what he sees. From fifteen yards away, he can see as clear as day between the slits in the men's jackets, the dull blue metal gleam of semiautomatic pistols. Roberto looks at the three Rangers standing at the entrance to the emergency room and subtly makes the sign of a gun with one hand as he points to the two couples and boys at the van. One Ranger acknowledges the signal from Roberto, says something into his radio microphone on his shoulder, then motions the other two Rangers to follow him. They approach the minivan, weapons already drawn and pointing at the suspects as Major John Brown and two other Rangers come running out the entrance with shotguns in their hands. Brown and his men completely overwhelm and take down the assailants before they can even respond or reach for a weapon.

Roberto feels a hand on his shoulder. With lightning speed, he wraps his arm around the other person's arm and throws him to the ground only to find he is looking into the face of his son Willito.

"Holy crap, Dad, what are you doing?"

Roberto quickly helps his son up and explains what is going on. Willito, also a law enforcement officer, heads over to the scene and asks Major John Brown if he needs any help. John lets his Rangers finish cuffing the assailants and taking the young boy to get treated for the dog bites.

He pats Willito on the back, "You to go take care of his wife, everything is just fine here because of your quick-thinking dad."

John then looks at Roberto and gasps, "Roberto, the next time you start talking to me about God and how He watches over us, and protects us, I'm going to be all ears. You just stopped one hell of a mess from happening."

Roberto's heart is pumping ten times faster than it is supposed to. He manages to get out, "*Gracious, A Dios.* God did save every one of us, didn't He?"

John smiles with glossy eyes. "He sure did. He did it with my good old friend, Chief Roberto Garcia."

Roberto and his son Willito walk into the birthing prep area of the hospital's maternity ward to find Isabella in a heated conversation with Carmen's doctor. "Dr. Kennedy, I know you are the doctor here, but I was an LPN for thirty-five years and I know what a breach looks like. This ultrasound is not showing anything but a healthy baby in the right position ready to be born," Isabella is yelling as she is pointing a finger to a monitor next to Carmen's bed.

"Mrs. Garcia, I am not going to stand here and have a retired nurse tell me how to do my job. It is my medical opinion that Carmen and the baby's lives are in danger, and that we need to do an emergency c-section immediately."

An older man in a doctor's smock walks into the area and looks straight at Dr. Kennedy. "Michael," he says, "there is way too much drama going on here. We just had an attempted witness assassination in emergency. I can't have all this yelling in my ward. What is going on?"

Dr. Kennedy is visibly stunned by the appearance of Dr. Keller, who is the head of the maternity ward at the hospital. "Dr. Keller, I thought you were out this evening. I have a distraught mother-in-law here who won't let me do my job and save this girl's life."

Dr. Keller looks over at Isabella and then to Dr. Kennedy and says, "Kennedy, this distraught mother-in-law is one of the finest maternity nurses I have ever worked with. Whatever she has to say, I think we should both listen to before any procedure is decided on."

Isabella grabs Dr. Keller's arm, drags him over to the viewing screen, and shows him the ultrasound taken earlier that day of Carmen. He takes a good long look at the screen, then takes his glasses off to rub the bridge of his nose and eyes with his index finger and thumb.

"Dr. Kennedy, have you completely lost your mind? There is nothing here to justify doing an emergency c-section on this woman."

Kennedy makes a mad dash for the exit only to run into Major Brown and another Ranger.

The Ranger grabs and holds the young physician as Brown says, "Dr. Kennedy, are you in some kind of a hurry? Maybe you are in a hurry to go get this!" He holds up the package with Dr. Kennedy's name on it and one hundred thousand dollars inside. The note inside reads, *It was necessary to not tell you everything. Get out of the hospital immediately and tell the police only that you barely escaped with your life. Hide the money and burn this note. I will contact you in a few days. —B*

He looks over at Roberto and Isabella and says, "Those gunmen Roberto just helped us apprehend had this package on them with some pictures of four people identified as "additional targets." John shows the Garcia family the four pictures of themselves.

"It looks like that cartel witness wasn't the only hit for those guys tonight. They were going to kill the four of you as well. Roberto, do you have any idea why?"

Dr. Kennedy starts to panic and exclaims that he had no idea that anyone was going to be killed, only that he was paid to detain the Garcia family for as long as he could here tonight. Major Brown asks the hysterical doctor, who hired him? Kennedy tells him the whole story about the casino owner across the border who almost killed him for a gambling debt and the mysterious Russian who showed up and bailed him out, then hired him for the job of detaining the Garcia's. The only name he had for them was Boris. John Brown was pretty sure that the casino owner they were talking about was Maximillian Manerez, the head of the same cartel that his witness was testifying against in three weeks. As for this Russian named Boris, he did not have a clue.

John looks at Roberto and asks if any of this makes sense. Roberto tells him that he does not know Maximillian, just that he has seen some news stories on him lately. And that the only Boris he knows of is a client of Jim Edwards, his in-law. He explains to John that Jim owns a wholesale operation for used cars near an auction in Pennsylvania and that Boris sells his cars through Jim's company. He says Boris is not the real owner of the company, but a little weasel named Yuri who is his nephew. Boris is a glorified salesman who has a lot of control over Yuri probably due to family ties.

Then a very alarming idea hits Roberto's head. "You know, Boris brought down some special ballet master from Russia to check out Danielle's recital tomorrow, and he invited Danielle and Jim with some of the older dancers for a cruise around the South Padre Island this evening. Isabella and I were going to go as well, but we got the call about Carmen's emergency and headed over here right away."

John Brown rubs his chin with his fingers in a thoughtful gesture and remarks, "It looks like someone went to extreme measures to keep you from going on that cruise, and then permanently get you all out of the way."

Same Day, Manheim, Pennsylvania

Barbara sits in Jacob's old office trying to come to terms with the fact that she had something to do with the death of this great man. Her iPhone Facetime indicator chirps. It's an unknown contact but she answers anyway. A very familiar, but older and harder face appears on the screen which she recognizes as Captain Marnia Gonzalez.

"I am sorry to startle you again Barbara, but Agent Yeager asked me to contact you and to ask you to hold tight there. He is having you picked up by a special transport to the Harrisburg Airport in a little while. He needs you in South Texas. I wanted to see your face so I called this way. It was so good hearing from you after all these years. I had no idea whether you were alive or dead."

Barbara starts to cry again and says she can't believe that Marnia could stand to look at her after she had an affair with her father. Marnia lets out a big huff and explains that her father was like any powerful man in the world who thought he deserved more than everyone else, and he had several other affairs after Barbara. Then she giggles and says, "Of course, none of them ever had him wrapped around their little finger like you did. I swear when it came to you, my poor father could not think straight."

"Whoever your "Obi wan" was for instruction in seduction, he taught you well."

Despite herself, Barbara laughs. Little Marnia was always a fun friend. She realizes just how much she missed taking care of her. Barbara walks around the office as she and Marnia reminisce about the better times they had, when Marnia catches a glimpse of a rather odd sign on the wall in Jacobs' old office. Marnia gasps and asks Barbara to back up and show her the sign.

The sign is a simple rectangle with a fancy frame around a white sheet with black letters on it "426 ADPL CDR 01\07\08, 06\07\90." Marnia asks Barbara what the sign means and why it's in Jacobs' office. Barbara explains to her that it is a designation code that belonged to Jacob Edwards when he retired from the Coast Guard in 2008. It was actually Jim who had the sign made and recently hung it up in Jacob's office. In Coast Guard speak, it showed that when Jacob was forced to retire because of Cozumel, he was next in line for the rank of captain, and was probably going to command one of the Coast Guard's newest security cutters. That sign shows the enormous fatherly pride that Jim has for his hero son.

Marnia gasps and exclaims "*Oh mi Dios! Es un milagro*" (Oh my God! It is a miracle). Barbara asks what is going on. Marnia tells her that she can't say for sure right now, but if she is right, it is the most extreme and extraordinarily wonderful thing that could have happened. Marnia again tells Barbara to wait there with the rest of the FBI and Police until the transport arrives, and that Chuck Yeager's people would fill her in on what is happening.

Houston Airport, Same Day

Since Natasha had Yuri pick up her father late last night at the airport in Houston and take him to handle some last minute business at Falcon Lake, perhaps the fatigue of not sleeping all night was why Yuri's behavior was less than favorable at the marriage license office. In spite of that, she sent him right back to Falcon Lake along with the documents to pick up Boris and bring him to Station Brazos.

Jim Edwards had decided to leave Thursday evening instead of Friday, so she knew he was already at the Garcia's house and would drive himself to Station Brazos to meet up with everyone to board the yacht.

On her way to the airport, Natasha uses the Bluetooth hands-free option in the little Mercedes C230 she rented to make a few phone calls. Satisfied that her father's special yacht and their friends from south of the border were all going to be in place by 7 p.m., she pulls into the short term parking garage and walks over to meet Alyeks at his gate.

Natasha had only met Alyeks a few times before, but had several conversations with him over the years. Being the head of all her father's interests in Europe, Natasha kept a tight control on people like Alyeks who needed more than wealth to motivate their loyalty. Through the crowd coming out of the secure part to the airport to luggage, she sees Alyeks, roughly six feet tall, one hundred seventy-five pounds—a very athletic looking middle-aged man. He could easily pass for someone fifteen years younger. She waves him to meet her at the luggage carousel for his flight. He immediately acknowledges her and heads over.

Natasha smiles as she analyzes Alyeks. She appreciates why he is so popular with his younger female students. Though no one accused him of being a pedophile, he was known to pursue relations with students as young as seventeen before. For that reason, her father left her strict orders to keep him on a very tight leash down in South Texas. Neither she nor her father would want to be put in the position of rescuing him from an angry Latino father who would not think twice about killing a man for inappropriate behavior toward his teenage daughter.

"Alyeks, it is good to see your plane is on time. Let's hurry. We have to meet the yacht rental agent in one hour."

Alyeks rolls his eyes, "Oh, so nice to see you too Natasha. Yes, my flight across the Atlantic Ocean in the middle of the night was horrible. You and your father sticking me in coach did not help much either." Natasha gives her best stone face to Alyeks and tells him to grab his luggage and follow her. Alyeks' luggage barely fits into the little Mercedes that Yuri rented for his cousin, but after some elaborate swearing in Russian, the unlikely couple manages to get his stuff packed into the small trunk.

They get on Interstate 69 from the airport into Houston and take Interstate 45 to League City. Alyeks immediately tries to bring up the availability of visiting his brother as soon as possible. Natasha, ready for that request, simply tells him that if everything goes as planned this evening, he would have his request and that there would be no more discussion on the matter.

They ride the rest of the way listening to music on an American country music station, which Alyeks finds he enjoys, much to his and Natasha's surprise. They arrive at Richman's Princess Charters rental facility a little before 2 p.m. in the South Harbor of League City. Natasha quickly reviews with Alyeks the logistics of the operation before entering the building to reassure herself that Alyeks would play his role adequately.

"I am your assistant. You may greet and make small talk with the associate, but leave all the logistics to me. We only need you to sign the paperwork as a representative of the Russian Ballet Academy, and then urge them to get on their way because we have to be at Station Brazos by 7 p.m. sharp."

Alyeks gasps. "I have no authorization to rent some high-priced yacht for the Russian Ballet. Are you mad?"

Natasha laughs her evil and vampish laugh, placing a soft hand on Alyeks' shoulder. She tells him that the officials at the academy will back up whatever action he takes in their name and that the yacht has already been paid for from her father's accounts. Alyeks, sufficiently pacified, gets out of the Mercedes and follows Natasha into the business office to meet with their representative. They are immediately greeted by an attractive woman of about twenty years when they enter the outer office. To Natasha's annoyance, this woman is completely unknown to her.

"Excuse me, but we are here to see Mr. Tom Richman, the owner of this facility. I am Natasha Rasmov, and this is Mr. Alyeks Yeshlton of the Russian Ballet."

The young lady smiles bigger and says, "Oh, this is such an honor, Mr. Yeshlton. I am Karen Richman, Tom's daughter. When I found out that you were chartering from us, I just had to talk Daddy into letting me handle the deal. After all, I am a ballerina myself and you are one of my biggest idols."

Oh my God, thinks Natasha, *if Alyeks tries hitting on this girl, I will give him bruises in places that will keep him from thinking that way for a long time.*

"I understand your excitement to meet Alyeks. We get that quite often, but we are on a very tight schedule and need to be at Brazos by 7 p.m."

Karen Richman, the high-society daughter of a very wealthy and powerful Texas businessman, is not accustomed to people talking to her like that and huffs as she barks back, "We have the best yachts in South Texas, and Mr. Yeshlton has charted our flag ship the *Princess Royale II*. I am sure we can accommodate all your needs."

Natasha ignores the snooty attitude and continues to ask pertinent questions regarding the charter, pretending not to notice Ms. Richman's desire to flaunt herself to Alyeks. Much to her surprise, Alyeks is not responding to the beautiful young lady's obvious fascination with him. On the contrary, he barely answers any of her questions. Natasha makes a mental note that maybe her father was wrong about him, and he can focus on the task at hand.

They spend the next fifteen minutes signing all the appropriate paperwork and meeting Captain Bliss, the yacht commander. As Karen is about to leave, she manages to place a flyer in Alyeks' hand and tells him that she is dancing in a *Swan Lake* production at her college in Houston next weekend and would love to have him as the VIP guest of honor. She kisses him on the cheek, ignores Natasha, says goodbye, and endeavors to make a lasting impression with the way she swaggers off the dock.

As they board, Natasha asks Captain Bliss two questions that pique Alyeks' curiosity; has the catering company she hired arrived yet, and is the Texas minister on board? The captain says "yes" to both questions. He tells her the minister is waiting in the ballroom and gives them a quick tour of the facility. He introduces them to Mr. Tom Wheeler, a robust, middle-aged, ex-Navy man who is the yacht's regular chef and social event coordinator, and excuses himself to the command deck to prepare to launch for Brazos.

Natasha's private caterers explained to Tom that his chef services were not needed and booted him out of his galley. He tells Natasha that if she needs his help with anything, just let him know. She thanks him and heads to the ballroom to check on the minister. On their way, Alyeks pulls Natasha aside and anxiously asks her who the devil is getting married. She tells him to calm down and that the whole reason for getting the Edwards out on this boat is so that Danielle will be forced to marry Yuri, her cousin, and make him the president of Edwards Auto.

"That is completely ridiculous. All they have to do when they are away from you, and…" It hits Alyeks like a ton of bricks. He leans against the wall and puts both hands on the sides of his head. "Danielle and her grandfather are not getting off this boat alive, are they?"

They are in a small hallway that goes from the dining room area to the banquet room. Natasha pulls a Walther PPK nickel-plated, semi-automatic from her pants and puts the barrel up into Alyeks' throat.

"Neither will you if you do not do exactly what I tell you."

Alyeks is shaken beyond his ability to cope and almost loses control of his bowels as he nervously shakes his head in compliance.

Natasha takes the barrel of her pistol and rubs it along the side of his face. She uses her tongue to lick the underside of his chin and neck as she whispers in his ear, "Besides, if you are a good boy, I can think of many ways to reward you that we both can find adventurous."

Alyeks rides the wall down to a seated position on the floor and begins to weep, broken by this very evil woman. Natasha looks at the sniveling coward, spits at him, throws her head and shoulders back, holsters the Walther inside her pants so that it is well hidden, and walks into the ballroom to brief the minister on what is expected of him this evening.

Rev. Billy Whitehall can hardly believe he is in this situation. He is one of the more popular pastors in the greater Houston area, and has an attending congregation of almost ten thousand. He grew up in southern Oklahoma. After divinity school, he married his childhood sweetheart and moved to the Houston area to be the youth pastor for the church for which he is now head pastor.

He is without doubt the most prosperous minister of his graduating class. His people adore him, and rightfully so, because he knows how dynamic he is in delivering his inspiring messages every Sunday. Why shouldn't young girls in his congregation look up to him and take care of his needs? David the King in the Old Testament had many wives, and so did others. Surely it wasn't sin for him to partake of the fruits of his own flock?

He had a special affection for that sweet, young, high school junior, Molly Brown. He was, after all, doing her a favor by rescuing her from the less-than-deserving boys who were clamoring after the many fruits of her pleasures. Besides, he always took care of his special favorites. He wrote them flowering recommendations to fine institutions of higher learning and even at times helped them get their first jobs after graduating college. Life was wonderful. His sweet wife never had a clue about any of his extracurricular activities and was as trusting and devoted as the day they married.

He thought he'd always been very careful and discreet about his regular rendezvous with Molly Brown after choir practice; so how could that evil snake-of-a-man, Boris, appear in his office late one Friday night a few months ago with graphic pictures of his private pleasure times with Molly? He knew that if anyone ever saw them, he would be utterly ruined.

Boris told Billy that he needed him to legalize a marriage at the end of the summer and to wait for further instructions. That is the only time that he had ever seen him. About two weeks later, he got a phone call from Yuri Sebastion, who informed him that he would be the groom in the upcoming union. Yuri provided Billy with all the necessary information about himself and the bride-to-be, Miss Danielle Edwards.

Rev. Whitehall later received a package in the mail that had a complete dossier on Danielle and Yuri, which also included several pictures and other pertinent background information. A few days ago, a man showed up at his office late at night demanding that the information he was sent be returned. By then, he pretty much had everything in his head, especially concerning the very beautiful Miss Edwards.

Billy remembers exactly who her late father is, the renowned former Coast Guard Commander Jacob Edwards, Hero of Cozumel all those years ago. He thinks to himself how that under any other circumstances, he would jump at the opportunity to perform the wedding ceremony for such a famous man's daughter. But right now, all he wants is to make this personification of evil, this Boris, happy so he can get back to his own little piece of heaven in Houston.

As he stands there gathering his thoughts, a stunning, dark-haired woman wearing expensive leather boots, tight-fitting black jeans and a white silk blouse enters the banquet hall from the opposite side. She walks straight up to him wearing a devilish grin as she extends her right hand and says, "Reverend Billy Whitehall, I am Natasha. I believe my father told you about me?"

Billy looks her up and down and sarcastically replies, "Oh yes, Natasha. I believe he said that I was to obey your every command without question."

Natasha is not at all taken aback by this self-righteous pig's attitude. On the contrary, this is very familiar ground and she knows exactly how to proceed. "Well, *Reverend,*

I believe that little Molly's dad is quite a large, brawny oil rig worker. He looks like he could break a scrawny little worm like you in half. So, it is quite clear that my father's instructions and your compliance to them are your only *grace* in this whole situation. Do you plan to be difficult or not?"

Billy knows he is owned. His shoulders droop as he looks off to the side and tells Natasha he will do whatever she wants. Natasha tells the reverend that there really isn't going to be a ceremony, but that he is to make sure the banquet room looks like a ceremony is going to take place. She flicks her head as if to say get busy, and turns to leave. As she heads toward the same door through which she originally entered, she spins and says, "You have about four hours before we get to Brazos Station, so have the room completely done by then."

Billy raises his arms in frustration and says, "You expect me to set up everything by myself? The officiating clergy shouldn't have to do anything like that at all!"

Natasha leans with one hand up on the side of the door and says, "Oh Billy, please, we had to lighten the staff on the boat in order to carry out our plans. I will see if the captain can spare you one of his two crew members, but if not, you're on your own."

Natasha walks back into the same little hallway where she left Alyeks groveling on the floor. As expected, he's still there. An idea hits her brain that tickles her fiendish funny bone. "Alyeks, my dear, in the banquet room next door you will find a Reverend Billy Whitehall of Houston Texas. He is endeavoring to get the room ready for Danielle and Yuri's blessed union. Please go help him. It will distract you from all the self-pity you are experiencing right now." She laughs. "You two have much in common. Both you and he have an appetite for women much younger than yourselves. Though his is a little more extreme than yours ever was."

Alyeks says nothing. He gets up and turns to the door Natasha is pointing at. "Oh, stop all this senseless pouting, Alyeks. When this is over, you will be taken to your brother's hospital where you will have a few days. Then you can go back to your lavish life at the ballet academy where you will never have to think about these peasants again." Still silent, he walks into the banquet room.

Natasha heads to the kitchen to check on the hired caterers. Two of the men are actually their own hired hands and an integral part of the plan. She finds them in the galley with seven others from a Houston catering company who are frantically scurrying around trying to prepare for the guests who will be on board in less than four hours. Natasha engages the man in charge and goes over some last-minute details for the wedding cake, and other items.

The caterer finds it kind of strange that everything is to be put in the banquet hall and locked up until just before the ceremony. Natasha tells him that there are going to be an excess of children from the bride's dance company, and she does not want any accidents to upset things. When she is done with him, she makes like she is leaving but glances at one of the men setting up and motions him with her chin to meet her out back.

Five minutes later, she stands at the rear of the yacht looking over her left shoulder out at the Gulf Bay. The Texas sun is just starting to dip in the western sky. The yacht is cruising full speed toward South Padre Island and Station Brazos. The big caterer she beckoned steps out of the cabin door behind her and moves up next to her. Natasha does not even look at him. "Are you and your partner ready for everything?"

The man answers in a very thick Spanish accent, "*Si*, I go to the engine room after we pick up the passengers. I subdue the engineer and make the engines ready. After guests are seated eating, I lock the other catering staff and boat's event coordinator in the walk-in refrigerator."

Natasha is pleased at his keen attention to the plan. "Remember, we are to do nothing to these people that a forensic expert could detect to counter our pirate attack ruse. We must proceed very cautiously here. My father has thought of everything and he is the very best at this kind of thing."

The man smiles and leans toward Natasha. "*Si, Señor* Rasmov is also the most generous *amigo* I have ever worked for. If you ever have need of me and my partner again, we are yours for the hire."

"And what about the cell phone jammer, was it delivered? Is it in place?"

The man explains that it is in place and the programmer said it was fixed up to allow all the numbers she sent to work but that it would jam everything else. He notes that with its range, no cell phones will work even in the vicinity of the boat. Users will think they have lost reception.

Natasha is satisfied that she can rely on these two as she tells him to get back to work and keep her updated. Out of the corner of her eye, she spots the yacht captain round the turn in a walkway and approach her.

"Was that caterer bothering you, Ma'am? I did not like the idea of bringing people we don't know on board, but the client Boris insisted. From what Mr. Richman says, he's got some deep pockets, so he got everything he wanted."

Natasha recognizes the genuineness of the captain's concern but knows she has to control the situation as well. "Captain Bliss, my father is of the opinion that his friend Jim Edwards' granddaughter's marriage to his beloved nephew Yuri deserves the very best, so that is his motivation for all the changes. The caterer was simply sent to me by his boss to ask if my father prefers steak or salmon. I told him steak of course, well done and spiced accordingly."

Captain Bliss is a bit surprised to learn that Natasha is the client's daughter. "I am sorry, Natasha. It is just that all this is a little confusing to me. The boat is chartered by the Russian Ballet Academy of Moscow, whom you and Alyeks work for, but the man paying all the bills is your father Boris. Why are we so secretive about the wedding when Danielle and her grandfather get on the boat? If this is a wedding cruise, then why the ruse with the great ballet instructor Alyeks Yeshlton coming to look at Danielle's dancers?"

Natasha is beginning to wonder if this yacht captain isn't a little too smart for his own good, but she and her father had already talked through this contingency and she is ready with an answer. "Captain Bliss, you force me to divulge everything. You see, my cousin Yuri has not yet proposed to his sweetheart Danielle. Although it is certain she will say yes. You see, she is already with Yuri's child. Neither she nor her grandfather knows about the proposal which is to happen at the dinner tonight. That is why Reverend Whitehall will be waiting in the banquet room for the *surprise*. I am sure a very happy bride will be married there tonight. My father thought that since Yuri impregnated his beloved before they were married, and that he is the only father Yuri knows, he should handle all the arrangements for the wedding." She quickly adds, "He is old fashioned in that way."

Captain Bliss rolls his eyes, whistles, and says, "Holy mackerel, if Commander Edwards were alive today and got his hands on your cousin Yuri, I don't think there would be much left of him to marry off."

Natasha is visibly shocked by the captain's response. "Did you know Jacob Edwards, Captain?"

Captain Bliss gives her a big grin. "Sure did. He was my commanding officer for three years in the Coast Guard. I was the communications officer on the *First Responder* when we rescued the cruise ship being attacked by those pirates. He's the greatest man I ever served under in my whole life. I cried like a baby when he, his wife, and mom died in that plane crash three years ago."

Natasha is now feeling the reassuring presence of the Walther PPK tucked in the back of her pants. "Yes, that was a great tragedy for my father as well, having worked with Jacob for many years in Manheim. Tell me, Captain Bliss, do you know Danielle or her grandfather Jim Edwards?"

"No, I am sorry to say that I have not had that pleasure yet, but am sure looking forward to it this evening."

Natasha is glad to abandon the idea that she needs to shoot this troublesome Captain Bliss in the head and dump his body in the ocean. Instead, she puts a provocative hand on his chest and asks him to keep his relationship to Danielle's father a secret, at least until Yuri proposes. Bliss sees the logic in not wanting to steal the young man's thunder and agrees. While standing on the deck, Natasha notices a very nice deep sea fishing seat with a full rig of polls and a high-powered harpoon rifle in a sleeve next to the seat. She looks at Captain Bliss. "Perhaps we should make this section off limits to the children. We would not want any unwelcomed accidents."

Captain Bliss acknowledges the potential danger and says he will section off the whole area for the cruise. Natasha always recognizes a good potential tool and wants to make sure of its availability if necessary. She thanks the captain and adds that if the bride and groom would like to spend some romantic time alone just after the ceremony, he should make sure they are allowed.

After making her rounds for three hours, Natasha is satisfied that all is set for the final stage of her father's plan. Captain Bliss announces on the ship's loudspeaker that they are about twenty minutes out of Brazos.

CHAPTER NINE
COMPLICATIONS

Same Night, Crossing the Bay in South Texas

Boris opens his eyes as he and Yuri cross the bay from Isabella to Padre Island on State Route 100. He looks down at his watch; it's 6:45 p.m. A sly smile appears on his wrinkled face. In a few moments, one of the only human beings in this world who has ever hindered him will be dead, and in a few hours more, all his plans will come together and he'll be on his way to being one of the most powerful underworld figures on the planet.

Boris has always been totally committed to the source of all his good fortune. During all those years of working for other people, killing for governments and crime bosses, he thought his employers were great powers to be served and by which to be rewarded. But he finally came to understand that the death he deals is his true master. It is the power of death that brings him everything he has and makes him everything he is. Death is permanent and irreversible. It solves every problem and rewards those who know how to deal it best. Boris is a willing servant of his master, death, and because of that he is rich and powerful. Even at seventy years old, he feels unstoppable. Not even a Bible-thumping maggot like Roberto Garcia will stand in his way for long.

Yuri pulls into the parking lot of Coast Guard Station Brazos and sees the bus containing Danielle and her Dance company, and a SUV rental sitting next to it with Jim Edwards inside. Then he sees something that is very disturbing to him. Next to the bus on the opposite side of Jim's SUV is a red Jeep Wrangler that belongs to Lt. Chris Rottanelli.

"Oh my God, Uncle Boris, that asshole Lieutenant who Danielle has been seeing is here. What do we do now?"

Boris looks at the Jeep and sneers at his nephew. "You are an imbecilic idiot to the thousandth degree. This is his station and he commands a patrol boat out of this port. Of course he would be here." Boris is tempted to draw the razor-sharp blade from his walking stick and decapitate the idiot sitting next to him who by some freak of nature and great curse is related to him. "This could work to our advantage. If the commander of the largest Coast Guard patrol boat in this area is with us, then the Coast Guard's response time to the scene will be even more delayed than we had hoped for."

Yuri, still frantic, practically yells at his uncle. "But if they walk on the yacht like a couple of lovebirds, then won't the crew think that something is off about my proposing to her later?"

Boris is shocked that Yuri's brain is actually capable of conceiving a valid concern. But he's still useless when the fluidity of an operation throws a snag like this—screaming and freaking out rather than coming up with solutions. He calmly reaches for his cell phone and calls Natasha to explain the situation to her. She listens and then proceeds to give her father additional information about the ship's captain that might help in the situation.

"So, Captain Bliss served under Jacob Edwards at Cozumel? That is interesting. Yes, if we can keep the captain and Rottanelli distracted until we are out to sea, I think this will work out wonderfully."

Natasha hangs up and walks up to the command deck where Captain Bliss is about to dock the *Princess Royale II* at Brazos Station.

"Captain, might I have a word?"

Bliss walks over and tells Natasha he is really busy at the moment, but before he can say any more, she tells him how her father would love to do some deep sea fishing tonight, and asks if he could arrange that. Bliss frowns and tells her that no one asked to fish on this trip so they did not get any licenses for the passengers.

"Is it possible that we can get the proper documents at Brazos, Captain?"

Bliss considers the request and tells her that it is Saturday evening after working hours and that there probably isn't anyone with enough authority to issue an afterhours deep sea fishing license at Brazos right now. Natasha slyly smiles and asks if the Lieutenant in command of the station's cutter would be able to help. Bliss says, "Well, yes. He can radio Corpus Christi and get the authorization, but everyone is probably off duty by now and not at Brazos."

"Well, Captain Bliss, we are in luck because Lieutenant Rottanelli is with the party that is about to board, and he is the commander of the patrol cutter stationed at Brazos."

"That's great," he says. "If the lieutenant has no problems handling this, then send him up to the command deck and he can use the radio phone to contact Corpus Christi from here."

Natasha thanks Captain Bliss for the quick thinking. Before she leaves, she steps a little closer to him and asks him in no uncertain terms not to let the lieutenant in on the proposal happening later that evening. She says that Rottanelli and Danielle used to be an item and it could get very awkward if he knew beforehand.

Bliss says sure and gets back to docking his ship. He had heard good things about the Brazos cutter commander and was looking forward to meeting him. Natasha gets back on the phone and calls her father to quickly explain the situation. Boris then says that he will handle the Edwards and the dance children, and that she should be ready to take Lt. Rottanelli to the command deck as soon as they board.

Danielle looks longingly out the window of the bus that picked them up at Jacob's Ladder about an hour ago. With all the commotion, she finally sees Chris' Jeep, and her heart starts to flutter with excitement. She brought Juan and ten of her older dancers along to meet Alyeks and go on the Cruise. The oldest is Juan at sixteen, and the youngest is a nine-year-old girl named Tabitha who barely speaks English. The children are so excited, and she's glad that Chris is here to be with her. His presence will keep people like Yuri and Alyeks from hitting on her, but that's definitely not the only reason she's glad he's here, not by a long shot. She sees Grandpa Jim's rented silver Ford Edge pull up. She tells Juan that he's in charge and gets up to leave.

Some of the fourteen and fifteen-year-old girls start teasing Juan. "Oh Juan, you are my favorite baby sitter," they wink and giggle at him.

Juan casts an exasperated look at Danielle who replies, "Suck it up tough guy. I'll be right back."

As she gets out, she sees Boris and Yuri walk over to her grandfather, so she decides to go see Chris first.

"Hey beautiful. Ready to show off the greatest dancers in the world?" Chris always knows what to say to make her feel special.

"Sure thing. We still have an opening in the third act. Want to try your luck?"

Chris laughs and says, "Oh sure and ruin Juan and the girls' chances of ever being recognized by the great

Alyeks Yeshlton of the Russian Ballet Academy? Not a chance. I would have about twenty-five moms ready to kill me before the recital was even over."

Danielle laughs and gives him a big hug and a kiss. They walk over to meet up with Grandpa Jim, Boris, and Yuri. Danielle gives Grandpa an affectionate hug and shakes Boris' hand, thanking him for setting this up.

"I had no idea your family had such big connections with the Russian Ballet, Boris."

Boris responds, "Alyeks was coming to the United States for some recruitment anyway. I just got him and his assistant to divert here after visiting Houston. All worked out well, did it not?"

Danielle acknowledges it is a wonderful turn of events. She continues to completely ignore Yuri which is no little source of awkwardness for all present.

To everyone's surprise, Yuri extends his hand to Chris and says, "I want to ask your forgiveness for my drunken behavior the other night at the grand opening. You acted in a most chivalric manner and I deserved the thrashing I received from you. I promise that it will never happen again."

Chris kindly returns the handshake and tells him that we have all made bad decisions while drinking too much, and the matter is forgotten.

Jim steps forward and says, "Well, now that that is out of the way, Boris and I were just talking, and we want to try our hand at some deep sea fishing later on tonight, but we need licenses to do it. The way I understand the laws down here, Chris, is that even though it's after hours, you as a cutter commander can call your sector command and get some kind of radio authorization for us?"

Chris nods. "Yes sir, that is correct. I just need to do it pretty quickly as my second-in-command is out on patrol right now."

Boris interjects and says, "I believe the yacht captain said that you could use the radio phone on his ship to conduct your business. Mr. Yeshlton's assistant, Natasha, is already waiting to take you to his bridge as we speak."

Danielle remembers the very beautiful woman from this morning and immediately offers to go with Chris, but Boris reminds her of her dance company, and she acknowledges that they are her first priority. She turns around to see eleven pairs of anxious eyes all staring at her , and she waves them off the bus. Everyone, including Juan, scrambles off as fast they can. They race to Danielle with one question on all their lips; "Where is Alyeks?"

Boris responds, "Follow me children, and I will introduce you to one of the most important people in all of ballet." His invitation actually has the opposite effect he expects. All the children freeze in place not really knowing what to do.

Jim Edwards has seen this effect Boris has on young people before. He steps in with his best grandpa smile and says, "Now, which one of you has ever seen the inside of a big old luxury yacht like that one over there?" Eleven heads shake in unison. "Well, come on! We better get cracking before it leaves us all here just gawking at it like of bunch of fat chickens."

Several giggles erupt and a couple of the little ones actually grab Jim's hands as they all board the *Princess Royale II* luxury yacht.

Boris smirks, *that's right my friend. Keep on bonding with the little brats; makes my plans work even better.*

Chris approaches the luxury cruise ship, thinking that somebody has some deep pockets. At the head of the ramp is a beautiful dark-haired woman. He notices her tight-fitting black jeans, high leather boots and white low-cut blouse and thinks, *oh man, if Danielle sees me staring at her, I will be in the doghouse for sure.*

"Hi, I'm Lieutenant Rottanelli. I'm supposed to meet with Alyeks Yeshlton's assistant, Natasha. Is that you?"

Natasha quickly analyzes the strapping young Coast Guard officer before her and comes to the conclusion that Danielle has excellent taste in men.

"Yes, I am Natasha. If you will follow me, I will take you to Captain Bliss so that we can get these deep sea fishing permits taken care of."

Chris walks up to offer her a handshake, but much to his nervous discomfort, she immediately grabs his arm, wraps hers around it, and leads him to the bridge. Captain Bliss is at the helm of the yacht when Chris and Natasha round the corner into the doorway.

"Permission to come aboard, Captain?" Chris says as he waits at the door.

Bliss gives his big ole Midwest smile and tells the Lieutenant and Natasha to come on in. "Sorry, Lieutenant, I can't shake your hand right now, I am down to a crew of two plus a chef…I mean event coordinator."

Chris tells Bliss that is quite all right; he'll just wait until they get out to sea to make the call. Chris turns to go back to the others, but Natasha insists that they wait there, and much to Captain Bliss' surprise she brings up that he served under Jacob Edwards in the Coast Guard. Chris is immediately intrigued and looks at Captain Bliss as he asks a bunch of questions about his relationship to the late commander.

"Well, gee," says Bliss, "that's my favorite subject in the whole world." He goes on to explain how he was Commander Jacobs' communications officer aboard the *First Responder* and that he was there for the Cozumel incident.

Chris walks up and pats Bliss on the back and says, "Yeah, I remember Jacob talking about you during that. He called you the nervous kid from Nebraska who just about crapped his shorts when he had to talk with the Vice Commandant of the Coast Guard."

Bliss gets a puzzled look on his face and casts a glance at Natasha, who is totally unreadable. His brows furrow as he looks Chris straight in the eye and says, "How did you know Commander Jacobs, Lieutenant?"

Chris tells him that he grew up in the same area as the Edwards and worked at their auto shop while in high school. He shares how Jacob helped him get into the Merchant Marine Academy at Kings Point and later into the Coast Guard.

Bliss shouts out, "What the hell!" as he turns to Natasha. "If he has all this background with the commander's family and used to date Danielle, then why would you and your father even consider taking this boy along for the whole fiasco that is about to happen?"

Chris looks at both of them, very confused, and says, "What do you mean 'used to date' Danielle?"

As fast as a black panther, Natasha pushes Chris over a table to her right and smashes Captain Bliss in the right temple with a left round kick using the steel covered tip of her leather boot. She sidekicks him in the chest with her right foot, puncturing his left shoulder with her heel, and draws her Walther PPK. She points the gun at a very astonished Lt. Rottanelli. Chris pulls himself to his feet and gawks at Natasha like he's just been attacked by an escaped lunatic.

"What the hell is your problem lady?" is all that comes out of his mouth before Natasha backhands him with the pistol and tells him to shut up or she will kill the captain, who is sprawled out on the command deck floor, bleeding and moaning.

"It would seem, Chris, that I have disabled our boat pilot. Therefore, I am promoting you to that position. Please take over the controls of this vessel before we run into something."

Chris stands there for a moment weighing his options, and decides that Danielle, Jim, and the children need him to do just that, so he goes to the helm and starts piloting the boat.

Natasha pulls out her cell phone and, using the Siri option, speed dials her accomplice who is in the engine room. She puts him on speaker so she can hold Chris at bay with her gun. It rings twice and a husky Spanish accent answers. "Yes, Natasha. What is it?"

"Are you finished with the engines yet?"

"*Si*, I just finished. The next time you turn them off, they will not start. If someone persists, it will start a fire down here that will hit the fuel tanks and blow the ship."

Natasha almost purrs in response. "Very good. Remember, the ship blowing up that way is plan B. Our Mexican friends should be at the rendezvous point in about two hours, and they are quite capable of destroying this vessel themselves."

"*Si, Señorita* Natasha, I know this. Is there something else you need?"

"I had to disable the captain and I have a very unreliable pilot at the moment. I need you up here as fast as possible. Tell your partner I will be down to help him and my father as soon as you and I have secured the helm and taken care of Captain Bliss and Lieutenant Rottanelli."

The hired thug says he's on his way as he steps over the lifeless body of the engineer he killed. Around the corner, he checks on the other crew member that he tied up and gagged. He found them down here drinking. They snuck away to enjoy a vintage bottle of vodka brought on board by the caterers at League City. *Funny*, he thought, *they slipped down here to get toasted and now that is exactly what is going to happen to them.* On his way to the command deck, he quickly texts his partner and Boris about the change in logistics and the need for him to go pilot the boat.

Danielle, Jim, Boris, Yuri, and the children are all seated around a very large banquet table with the catering crew as the event coordinator serves them their meals. The large Spanish man who talked to Natasha earlier that evening feels a vibration in his pocket and steps back into the kitchen to read the text from his partner. Ascertaining the situation, he steps out into the dining hall to see if Boris has gotten the message as well.

Boris is looking at his cell phone. When he looks up, he scans the room to locate the caterer who is working for him, nods in acknowledgement that he has gotten the message, and gives him the prearranged sign that it is time to get Tom, the event coordinator, and the rest of the Houston caterers locked up in the walk-in so they can get the hidden guns out and proceed to secure the ship. Boris looks down at his watch. It is 7:50 p.m., ten minutes until they reach the coordinates. He finds great satisfaction in knowing Chief Roberto and his family have finally met their compliance to his will, and encourages himself with the knowledge that nothing can now stand in his way.

*   *   *

Roberto and Isabella are still talking to Major John Brown when his cell phone rings at 7:52 p.m.

"Hello, this is Roberto Garcia."

"Chief Roberto, I don't know if you remember me. I'm Chuck Yeager. I was a good friend of your son-in-law, Jacob Edwards."

"Chuck, of course I remember you. You were Jacob's best man at his wedding. This is not a very good time to talk. I am with a Texas Ranger Major and somebody just tried to kill my family."

"I'm glad you're safe. They're trying to kill Danielle and Jim too. We tried to call them earlier, their cell phones must be disabled."

"I know," Roberto says, "I tried to call them too."

Chuck tells him that he is now the deputy director of the Philadelphia FBI and that he is on his way to arrest Yuri Sebastion and detain his uncle Boris for questioning concerning money laundering, murder, and conspiracy to commit murder.

Chuck gives Roberto the complete story he knows, and Roberto fills Chuck in on what transpired in Rio Grande City at Starr County Hospital in the last hour. Chuck is shocked to learn that Jim, Danielle, all those children, and Lt. Rottanelli are on the yacht with those murderous bastards.

"Are you sure they are already out in the Gulf?" Chuck asks.

Roberto chokes up when he says, "I am afraid so. They boarded at least an hour ago."

Major Brown can tell that his friend Roberto is pretty shaken up and motions him for the cell phone.

"Deputy Director Yeager, this is Major John Brown of the Texas Rangers. How can we help?"

Yeager and Brown talk for about five minutes. John will coordinate with the Coast Guard sector Corpus Christi, and Yeager will contact Captain Marnia Gonzalez of the Mexican Anti-Cartel Task Force. Together, they are going to send out everybody that they can contact to find that yacht.

Captain Larry Phillips is working at his desk when his office phone rings. "Captain Phillips, Sector Corpus Christi. May I help you?"

"Captain, this is Major John Brown of the Texas Rangers." He proceeds to tell Captain Phillips the whole story including what they pieced together about Boris' plans to somehow force Danielle to marry Yuri Sebastion and sign over Jim Edwards' business to him. Larry is especially astonished about the whole cartel money smuggling scheme that has been going on for so many years.

"Major, my predecessor Will Harrington runs the entire customs office in Brownsville. How could he miss something this big and for this long?"

"Captain, that is one damn good question."

Brown makes a note in his book about that little piece of info. They agree that the more pressing issue is to find that yacht and rescue those people.

"Major," Phillips says, "Lieutenant Rottanelli had the night off but his second-in-command, Lieutenant junior grade Wallace, is on patrol in those waters. He is the closest we have right now. I will contact him and get him looking for the yacht as soon as I end this call."

"Sounds good to me," the Major responds. "Roberto and Isabella are pretty shaken. I am going to fly them to Brazos in the county copter; we should be there in thirty minutes."

Deputy Director Chuck Yeager is seated next to Barbara in a federal FBI Cessna jet flying toward a small airfield in South Padre Island. He fills Barbara in on everything she could not catch from listening to his conversations.

"Chuck," she cuts in, "we have to find them quickly. Boris will not hesitate to kill every person on that yacht to get what he wants or to avoid being caught. He couldn't do this without a lot of help and I know how he operates. He has his own people on that yacht and has more help coming, probably disguised as pirates coming up the Gulf Coast from Mexico."

She also tells him to be on the lookout for Boris' private yacht; a modified, revved-up Millennium 140, painted dark gray, and equipped with military stealth technology and weapons. He will undoubtedly have that standing by somewhere. Chuck gets back on the phone with Captain Phillips and gives him the additional info. Phillips gets on the radio phone and dials the code for the new security cutter that now patrols this part of the Gulf.

"Maelstrom here. What's up, Larry?"

"Alex, we have a serious problem brewing near South Padre Island."

Larry tells Captain Alex Maelstrom the story and asks how long it would take him to get there at top speed.

"Captain," Maelstrom says, "if that damned son-of-a-bitch lays one hand on the commander's daughter, there won't be enough of him left to identify the body. I can be there in two hours."

Larry disconnects the line, sits back and thinks to himself how there were times that he was jealous of Jacob Edwards. The great Hero of Cozumel had everything going for him. Then Jacob wrote that stellar recommendation on his record and told the commandant that Larry should be put in command of the *First Responder*.

That was right at his recommissioning time. His then wife wanted him to leave the Coast Guard and use all his training to get a high paying job in the private sector, but he refused to quit. That was the beginning of the end of his marriage and the start of some major setbacks in his career.

The *First Responder* got another commander instead, a full captain. Maelstrom became the executive officer, and Larry took a desk job for a few years while he sorted out his personal life. He actually made the rank of Commander while working Sector New Orleans. The vice president of the United States, who was then the commandant, called him up and offered him Sector Corpus Christi and a promotion to Captain. During that time, he really kept close ties with Jacob and his family. He even went to Manheim for Christmas a few times. That's when Danielle started calling him Uncle Larry.

He gets on the phone and calls his sector's helicopter hangar. "Chief, this is Captain Phillips. I want you to prep the emergency rescue copter and get flight clearance to Brazos. We need to be there in one hour." In his heart, Larry knows he will do everything humanly possible to get Jim and Danielle out of this mess.

Captain Alex Maelstrom never got used to the fact that he commanded the ship that was supposed to go to Jacob Edwards. He did his damnedest to live up to the legacy of the finest officer under whom he had ever served. He thinks back to the last time he saw Jacob. It was at an All-Academy Ball held in Philadelphia six years ago. Jacob was there with a young Kings Point Midshipman 1st Class who was graduating that year and then getting commissioned by the Coast Guard. The boy didn't have a date, so Jacob and Mary decided to go with him for company.

Alex loved the effect Jacob had on the brass. There were a lot of retired commanders in the Coast Guard, but there was only one known as "The Commander", and that was Jacob Edwards. The moment he walked into the banquet room, two admirals and a captain jumped to their feet to greet him. Maelstrom, who was a brand new Commander out of grad school in Philadelphia, remembers he also jumped up to greet him. Jacob took the opportunity to introduce the young Kings Point midshipman to them; Chris Rottanelli.

Captain Maelstrom's intercom buzzer sounds, and it is his deck officer. "Sir, that cutter you told us to look for just pinged our radar."

"Intercept at best speed. I'll be right up."

As they approach the mysterious cutter in open waters about an hour and a half south of Padre Island, Captain Maelstrom can't help but get a sense of *déjà vu* when they open fire on his ship with Goon Guns. He thinks to himself, *are these guys for real? Do they ever try anything different?*

Something explodes next to the cutter. "Captain!" the deck officer yells, peering through his night vision binoculars. "They're launching Bangalore torpedoes at us too!"

He orders his gunnery officer to target the launcher, and the ship's rudder and propeller areas. With the upgrades in aiming and radar that the new security cutters have, every shot is a direct hit and the other ship is quickly disabled. He sends a security crew to go take over the ship as he calls the Navy and asks for help in securing the assailants. Once he knows the situation is under control, he orders his second-in-command to proceed to Padre Island to look for the yacht that Commander Edwards' daughter is on. A few of Alex's crew actually served with or under Commander Edwards back in the day, so there is a lot of enthusiasm in carrying out the order.

Chuck Yeager makes one last call before he and Barbara land at Padre Island. Marnia answers after the second ring. They discuss the situation for about five minutes and decide that she needs to be there as well.

"I am in the Brownsville area, Mexico side of the border, checking on a lead connected to the Maximillian Manerez Cartel and Yuri's money smuggling operations."

She tells Chuck that she can helicopter to the nearest Mexican naval base and commandeer a *CB90 HMN Polaris-class* interceptor patrol boat and be in the area in about two hours. Chuck says he will keep in contact with her by phone and will make sure that Captain Phillips knows a Mexican patrol boat will be in U. S. waters in a few hours. Marnia disconnects.

She is nervous about the ongoing situation on that yacht with that snake Boris. All she can think about is how Jacob saved her life from the Jamaican all those years ago. She heard him tell someone that Marnia reminded him of his own daughter. She had met Danielle Edwards only once at the funeral. She is totally committed to seeing that not a hair on the head of the Hero of Cozumel's daughter is going to be harmed.

She decisively barks orders to her military subordinates to get her a transport copter to the naval base and have a CB90 fueled and waiting for her when she arrives. Over the years, people in the Mexican military learned that when The Cartel Crusher was on the hunt, you had two choices; help or get out of her way.

Roberto and Isabella sit next to each other at Station Brazos. Roberto thinks about how much he really loves this place. Having been the commanding chief for so many years, he knows every nook and cranny like the back of his hand. He looks out at the dock where he and Jacob stood talking next to the *First Responder* all those years ago when they responded to the cruise ship incident. It dawns on him that it is exactly the thirteenth anniversary of that night they both went to Cozumel.

He takes his wife by both hands and looks into her eyes, "That night all those years ago, for the first time I saw our son-in-law ask God to help him and to protect both our crews. He told God that he was not into combat, but that he couldn't stand to let bullies get away. I don't pretend to understand what caused Jacob to throw that Jamaican off the ship that night, but I know that God protected him, his crew, and mine just like he prayed.

"Isabella, we have prayed. God is bigger than anything, and He is right there with Danielle, Jim, Chris, and those children. There is one thing that I am positive of right now; we need to believe that Danielle finds the strength to fight back. If she does, they will all be okay."

Major John Brown steps up and tells the Garcias that Captain Phillips and Deputy Director Yeager are on their way to Brazos. He tells them that Lt. Rottanelli's boat will be there in about thirty minutes to pick everybody up and go look for the yacht; and he tells them that Captain Maelstrom is in command of the new security cutter patrolling this part of the Gulf, and that he also is on his way. Last of all, he tells them that Captain Marnia Gonzalez of the Mexican Anti-Cartel Task Force is racing up the coast in one of Mexico's new *CB90 HMN Polaris Interceptor* patrol boats to help.

"Geez, I know about her," John adds. "They call her 'The Cartel Crusher'. She's not someone to piss off or mess with."

Roberto tells the major that Marnia was the little girl whose life Jacob saved back in Cozumel.

"Well," he says, "she's officially part of the team. Captain Gonzalez and deputy director Yeager are part of a joint task force investigating Yuri Sebastion's money laundering and smuggling operations."

Isabella looks at her husband and then at John. "John, you told my husband back at the hospital that the next time he brings up God, you would be all ears. Would you pray with us here right now for this whole situation to be done and have a positive conclusion?"

John gulps and says, "Sure, Isabella. I'll pray with you and Roberto."

Chief Roberto, his wife Isabella, and Major Brown grab each other's hands, bow their heads and pray right there on the dock of Station Brazos for the safe return of all their loved ones on that boat out in the Gulf somewhere.

Chapter Ten
The Wedding Present

Princess Royale II, Out to Sea

Danielle is getting more and more anxious by the minute about how long it is taking Chris to get back from the command deck with the deep sea fishing authorizations. She looks over at Tom, the event coordinator, to ask if he could check on him, but just then, from the side door, Alyeks Yeshlton of the Russian Ballet Academy steps in with Natasha and everyone in the whole room stands and erupts in applause.

Natasha looks at everyone with a huge smile that shows off her pearly white teeth framed by her very red and full lips. "I am sorry for the delay, but Lieutenant

Rottanelli was getting the authorization for the deep sea fishing when Captain Bliss became quite ill with what looks like some type of nausea. We have him resting in the captain's cabin, and Chris, being a very experienced and licensed boat pilot, has agreed to handle the rest of the cruise, at least until the captain is feeling better."

Danielle looks over at her grandfather —who is not buying any of this either — and stands to say, "I think I will go up and check on Chris and see for myself what is going on."

One of the caterers working for Boris steps out with a couple of Uzi machine pistols. He tosses one to Natasha, and they both point them at the whole group.

Tom, the event coordinator gasps and yells, "What the hell is going on here?" as he rushes the caterer.

In an unbelievably quick flash, Boris is on his feet. He turns and cracks the man on the side of the neck just below his ear and above his jaw bone with his walking stick. Tom hits the floor face first, totally unconscious. Boris darts over to Natasha who reaches behind her with her free hand and gets out her Walther, still in its holster, and gives it to him.

"Don't worry, Father, I cleaned it this morning. It is in perfect working order."

Father, Danielle thinks, *that makes sense*. Seeing them stand next to each other, she now realizes why Natasha seemed so eerily familiar this morning at the notary clerk's office.

Boris directs his gaze at Yuri and says, "Don't just sit there like an idiot, go to the galley and get a gun."

Yuri silently gets up, looks over at Danielle with the most impish smirk on his skinny little face, and runs to the galley.

Boris glances at his hired hand and, with a questioning shrug, nods his head toward the unconscious event coordinator. The man answers, "He refused to follow me back to the kitchen with the others. He was very stubborn; I did not want to make a scene."

"That was a wise choice," Boris says as Yuri steps out of the kitchen with an Uzi in his hands. Boris tells him to go make sure the reverend is ready in the cathedral.

Jim Edwards, a bit confused and stunned by what is unfolding before him, finally jumps to his feet and says, "What's going on here with all these guns, Boris? You're scaring the children, and quite frankly, me too."

Boris belts out an enormous evil laugh, and Natasha joins in. They look at each other as if it is the funniest thing they have ever heard in their lives.

"Oh, Jim Edwards," Boris says, "you are the most stubborn man I have ever met in my life. I never thought I'd ever meet a rich man who could not be bought with more wealth until I met you, you stupid cowboy. If you just would have sold me Edwards Auto all those years ago when I made you that very generous offer, you would now be a wealthier man, who still had a wife, a son, and a daughter-in-law with you today."

The color drains out of Jim's face as he plops down in his chair feeling twice as old as when he stood up. "What are you saying Boris? That you…you killed my family? Why?"

"For starters, Jim, it's cost me ten times more to kill your family and to arrange this crazy little escapade tonight as it would have cost me to just buy you out; for that alone, you are going to suffer before you die."

Boris, irritated by the whimpering and crying of the children in Danielle's ballet company, all huddled up close to her and Juan, tells Natasha to do something about the whiny brats.

"Okay," she says, "I'll take them to the banquet room cathedral and we'll wait for you there."

Danielle is immediately on her feet, threatening to bash Natasha's face in if she touches one child. Natasha is genuinely amused. She grabs the youngest girl in the company and points her gun at the child.

"And after I kill this one and the next, what will your brave response be, hey?"

Danielle stares, unable to answer. Natasha tells Alyeks, who has not moved from her side the whole time, to help her with the children. Juan bucks, like he wants to fight, but Danielle puts her hand on his wrist and tells him that she doesn't think they want to harm the children, and to go with them.

Natasha laughs and says, "How very perceptive for a self-important debutante. You're right. We have other needs of these children that you—"

"That's enough, Natasha," Boris interjects. "What of the Coast Guard lieutenant and the boat captain?"

"The captain is quite incapacitated and Lieutenant Rottanelli is very secure in the locker off the captain's cabin. Our man is now piloting the yacht and we should be at the rendezvous point any moment."

Boris is pleased with the information and dismisses Natasha, Alyeks and the children. As they depart the room, Alyeks catches Danielle's eyes and mouths the word "sorry" to her. She replies with her middle finger.

"Now where were we, Jim?" Boris says, "Oh yes. You see my dear friend, I am not a family advisor to my ridiculously stupid nephew, Yuri, as I have let on all this time. Although he is very dumb and unreliable at times, he does in fact work for me and always has. My actual business involves the cleansing and-or transporting of money for major crime syndicates, cartels, and mafia that operate on the East Coast."

Boris goes on to explain that the traditional way of money laundering for crime is a somewhat slow and expensive process, and the more efficient way is to get the cash out of the United States and to Mexico or South America, where the owners are much freer to enjoy its use. The problem has always been the transporting itself.

Many schemes in the past have been tried and found out, like using buses, or college students going across country or the occasional trip over the border. Law enforcement, especially throughout the mid and south west, started collecting and keeping any large amounts of cash they found with anyone. Half the time, it was not even a crime related fund. Then Boris came up with a plan that has been exceptionally profitable. Why not use the auto auction and the transporting of sold wholesale vehicles to move the money?

Jim moves forward in his chair, puts his right hand under his chin, and leans on his elbow. "So that's why you have been interested in Edwards transport services and have been bribing Bob Billings."

Boris is astonished. "You knew about Bob's involvement?"

Jim huffs. "I knew that you and Yuri were bribing him. I just thought it was so that he would always make sure your cars got shipped first. I didn't know he was helping you transport dirty money in them."

Boris smiles at Jim. "I never thought you were stupid Jim, just a little shortsighted and way too sentimental for your own good."

Jim jumps out of his chair and slams his fist on the table as he yells at Boris. "And for that, you kill my wife, my son, and his wife? You bastard!"

Boris brandishes the Walther PPK and says, "If I were you, I would be a little concerned about the children in the next room. In fact, I think it is time we joined them."

Yuri and the hired caterer motion for Jim and Danielle to get up and go to the door that leads to the other banquet room down the small hall. As they are walking through the hall, they feel the engines go silent and the boat starts to slow down, then the sound of the dropping anchor. Boris hears his cell phone chirp with a message. He looks at Yuri gond says, "We are at the proper coordinates. It will be another hour and a half before our friends from Mexico get here, plenty of time to finish our business deal with the Edwards."

As they enter the next room, Danielle and Jim are completely stunned to see that the whole hall is decorated and set up like a wedding chapel. There in front, standing in clergy robes, is a man that Danielle has seen on TV. She remembers one Sunday morning a few months ago when she missed Bible fellowship at Grandpa Roberto's, she decided to try church TV from Houston. She came across a church service being broadcast from this man's parish, Rev. Billy Whitehall. She really liked the choir and felt that he had a powerful speaking voice, but she did not find much substance in his message and never listened to him again.

Boris tells Yuri to go to the groom's side of the room and has Danielle and her grandfather go to the bride's side. "Now, I am not going to force you two to go through the pains of taking any vows. I did, however, have to make sure that any crime scene investigators that recover the remains of this ship will clearly see that a wedding did indeed take place here."

"Natasha, do you have the license and the business contract with you?"

Natasha walks over to a satchel on a table and hands the contents to her father.

"Thank you my dear. Now, let us proceed..."

Danielle is beside herself as she looks at Yuri and sneers. "If you think that I am going to sign a marriage license with this creepy little worm, you're about three nuggets short of a happy meal, pops. Go to hell."

Natasha can't hold back how tickled she is with Danielle's tirade. "Oh, Danielle, believe me, I share your sentiments toward my cousin Yuri. But don't worry, you have already signed the marriage license. It only needs the signature of a licensed Texas clergy, which we just so happen to have right here."

Danielle remembers how awkward the whole situation was in the marriage license office that morning. The ruse of getting Edwards transporter documents signed and notarized made perfect sense. With the speed of a wild cat, she lunges at Yuri, slaps the Uzi down to the ground and hook kicks him in the temple, knocking him out cold.

Natasha, caught off guard, quickly collects her faculties and fires one shot into a nearby vase, disintegrating it. She threatens Danielle with her Uzi, backing her down.

"Alyeks," Natasha orders. "Pick up Yuri's weapon and guard her." Still holding her own weapon up, she says, "Danielle Edwards, I see that you are every bit the daughter of the Hero of Cozumel, I will no longer underestimate you."

Boris glares at his daughter. "Natasha, you know I despise that reference to that boy scout cowboy of Jim's. Please refrain from using it in my presence."

"Of course, Father." Natasha grabs the arm of the petrified Rev. Billy Whitehall and pulls him over to the table next to her father.

Boris opens the satchel that she brought him earlier, sternly looks at the man before him and says, "Now Rev. Whitehall, if you would be so kind as to sign this marriage license so that we can get on with the business at hand."

Billy does not hesitate. He grabs the pen from the table and signs the document. Boris looks at Danielle and his unconscious nephew laying on the floor and a gives a wry smile. "I believe the good Reverend has now pronounced you man and wife."

By this time, Alyeks is standing next to Danielle with an Uzi pointed at her head and his finger on the trigger. "Please, Danielle. Do not cause any more trouble. He will have my brother killed if I do not do what he says."

Jim looks over at his granddaughter and shakes his head in a solemn *no* to forestall any more outbreaks by her. Danielle, overwhelmed, drops into a chair close to the altar, and starts to cry. Clearly enjoying everything going on around him, Boris gives an excited wave to his daughter and tells her to bring Jim over to the table. He has his caterer bring over a couple of chairs so he and Jim can sit. They both take seats opposite each other at the table. He pulls another document from the satchel and gives it to Jim.

"Now that the happy couple are legally wed, Jim, let us discuss their wedding present. As an excited grandfather, out of the love in your heart for this blessed union, you are going to sign over complete control of Edwards Auto to the now Mr. and Mrs. Yuri Sebastion. I, on the other hand, have been authorized by Yuri's family, of which I am anonymously head, to gift them, as a couple, all holdings of Sebastion Enterprises. I believe this actually accomplishes a life time goal for you Jim. Your company, or former company, will become the largest independently owned automobile wholesale company in the entire world."

Jim rolls his eyes and glares at Boris. "You know this is all worthless. Once we get to the mainland, I will just dispute everything in court and even if you somehow get away, your whole operation will be ruined."

"My dear Jim," Boris shakes his head. "I've already told you that I am going to make you pay before you die, and mentioned authorities will find the remains of this boat. What makes you think that either you or Danielle will ever see dry land again?"

Jim remains calm. "If you're just going to kill us, why should I sign those ridiculous papers then?"

Boris looks over at his daughter. "Natasha, darling, please take the littlest girl over there outside to the deck, put a bullet in her head, and throw her body overboard."

Danielle flies out of her chair and lunges at Natasha screaming frantically, but is tripped by Alyeks and held down with an Uzi to her head. Jim stands straight up and like a bullwhip cracks Boris in the mouth with a right cross that sends the seventy-year-old Russian assassin to the floor in his chair.

"You take one step toward that little girl, Natasha, I will force your father to kill me right here, and then none of this will work, will it?"

Boris sits up, helped up by the caterer as he rubs his jaw. He pulls the razor-sharp blade from his walking stick and places the sharp edge against Jim's throat. As soon as it touches, a small trickle of blood begins to flow. "You are going to pay dearly for that, my old friend."

Jim is as calm and cold as Boris when he says, "I told you, I will force you to kill me and then none of this will work. The blade is at my throat and if anyone makes a move toward a child, I'll cut my own damn head off without signing your fucking papers. Your move, Boris."

Boris withdraws his blade, sits back down, and sighs long and deep. "Jim you are a worthy adversary after all. Let's be reasonable here. You and Danielle are going to die tonight. There is no getting around that. But these children do not have to meet the same end. They can be saved if you cooperate."

"Okay, Boris, I'll bite. What do you have in mind? Because you obviously are going to sink this boat, and I don't think you want to take a bunch of kids along on your escape boat, do you?"

Boris is becoming more and more intrigued by Jim's quick grasp of reality. "Well, for starters, for this ruse to work, Yuri, Natasha, and I have to appear as survivors of this voyage. The children know too much so they can never go home, but I have a group of people pressing toward our location as we speak. They have the means of profiting from, shall we say, their worth in certain markets."

Jim is flabbergasted. "Are you kidding? The only way to save their lives is to turn them over to human traffickers to be sold as slaves?"

"Yes, Jim. That is their only option for life. Think about it. I already have the marriage certificate, and though it legally may take years, I will eventually control Edwards Auto. In the meantime, it will be business as usual until I do. By making the transition easier, you will at least save these children's lives."

Jim is visibly broken by Boris' logic as he grabs the papers to sign, but then gets an idea. He puts the pen down. "While getting on board," he says pointing to the door, "I saw two motorized lifeboats with emergency supplies in them. Put one in the water, put the children in with the event coordinator to pilot the boat, tell your friends where to pick them up, and I will sign your damn papers. That way, I know you won't back out on your word and kill them with me and Danielle." Jim looks over at Danielle who, between sobs, nods her head in agreement to her grandfather's plan.

Boris looks thoughtfully at Natasha who just shrugs her shoulders. "That is a workable plan, Father."

"Okay Jim. We will do it your way. Now please, sign the papers."

Jim pushes the papers back. "I'll sign when the kids are in the boat. Not before."

"You must not try my patience too much, Jim. You really have no idea who, or what, you are dealing with."

Jim stares Boris down eye-to-eye as he very slowly rises to his feet. "I know exactly what I am dealing with; the man who blew up a plane full of innocent people just so he could kill my wife, my son, and his wife. The man who attacked a cruise ship full of innocent people that led to the death of twenty of them, just so he could get a pop shot at my son. No, I think I know exactly what I am dealing with; a murdering coldhearted bastard who is so sick with ambition and greed that he couldn't see the light of day if he tried."

Boris' fuming eyes drill into Jim with a rage that petrifies the entire room. Natasha steps up, places her hands on her father's shoulder and whispers into his ear, "If you kill him before he signs, there is too big of a chance that none of this will work and we will be back to square one. Just humor him, Father. You can enjoy killing him later."

Boris looks into his daughter's beautiful eyes, pauses, and turns back toward Jim, "Okay, Jim. Let's get the children in the boat, but the event coordinator stays with us. We will let Captain Bliss take the youngsters in the boat. He is slightly incapacitated at the moment, but knows considerably less of what has transpired here than the other man. Those are my terms."

Jim sits quietly thinking.

"Natasha," Boris says. "Is the captain conscious yet?"

"Yes Father, but he does not have the use of his left arm and is probably suffering from concussion."

"He will have to do." Boris points to Juan. "Perhaps that young man over there can help with the piloting of the boat."

Jim accepts the deal and stands with the rest of the people in the room as Boris' caterer, and Alyeks, and Natasha start to herd everyone toward the back door.

During all the commotion and confrontations, Rev. Billy Whitehall, with practiced quiet stealth, slank to the far back end of the room where he disappeared in the shadows. As the children travel through the dark hall, he waits and steps up behind the last girl, the older one in the dance company, wraps his hand around her mouth and flashes the blade of his sharp pocket knife in her face as he pulls her into a small utility room to the side. He takes the blade that he keeps on his person and has used in similar circumstances in the past, and holds it at her neck. He explains that he doesn't want to hurt her, but she must be absolutely quiet or he will cut her throat. He asks her if she understands. She nods, and he slowly removes his hand from her mouth but keeps the knife at her throat.

"Now that we understand one another, I want you to realize that I am doing this because I can see that Boris has no intentions of letting me live tonight. I don't think he is going to let any of you live either. So, you and I can keep each other company as this whole thing plays out. Who knows, maybe if we stay quiet, an opportunity will present itself and we can escape together."

The girl is barely sixteen, but she is not stupid and she can see the predator in Billy's eyes. She knows what he is after but is too terrified to do anything about it, so she just nods her head.

The rest file out to the back of the luxury yacht where the two life boats hang next to the fishing platform and the access step ladder that descends to the ocean for small boats or for swimming. Boris' caterer and Tom handle getting one of the lifeboats unhinged and lowered into the water next to the access ladder. Natasha and the other caterer who was piloting the boat, appear around the corner, propping up a disoriented Captain Bliss who is wearing a makeshift sling fastened together from an old torn shirt. There is also the stain of blood on his shirt where Natasha embedded her heel in his shoulder.

As they walk by Danielle, he stops and looks at her with solemn and dazed eyes. "I served under your father at Cozumel. I am so sorry that I failed to help you. Please forgive me."

Danielle touches his face and cups his cheek in her palm. "I remember Daddy talking about his wide-eyed, over-zealous communications officer. He really loved you. This is not your fault. Remember that."

Natasha pushes Danielle's hand away while mocking her. "Oh, you poor little darling."

They lower Bliss into the lifeboat, then Juan gets in and helps the rest of the girls board, getting them all seated and fastened in their life jackets. Bliss tells Juan how to start up the one horsepower outboard motor and gives him instructions on how to shove off from the yacht. When they get out from under the lights of the yacht it is hard to see them because it is nighttime on the ocean and pitch black.

Back inside, Boris directs his attention to Jim, slaps the papers a few times with his open palm and says, "I have lived up to my end of the bargain. The children are off the boat. Now, Jim, please keep your end as well."

Jim takes a pen from Natasha, walks over to the table where Boris sits, grabs the papers, and signs them all. "I don't know what good these are going to do you. Even if

I am dead, don't you think that the authorities are going to wonder how you so conveniently have them with you after the destruction of this boat?" Boris gives a genuine sign of appreciation for Jim's intelligence by patting him on the back. He tells him he must have learned all this attention to detail by being the final detail guy in his line at the shop all those years.

"You are correct to think it would be a little too convenient to find all this paperwork with me when we are rescued. That is why the papers and marriage certificate will be found in the wreckage of this boat, inside this." Boris holds up a stainless steel briefcase with a label that reads "Fireproof & Waterproof up to 100M." "This will be found by the crime scene investigators sometime after this evening."

Jim shakes his head as he throws his hands up in exasperation. "Okay, Boris, what's next?"

Chapter Eleven
Fight!

***Princess Royale II*, Anchored at Sea**

Chris is working his hands out of the zip ties. He is still in disbelief about how fast the whole thing went down. That crazy woman almost killed Captain Bliss, and then when the other thug showed up, they put a piece of duct tape over his mouth, zip tied his hands behind his back and his ankles together. Then they locked him in Captain Bliss' cabin closet. He had the presence of mind to tighten up his fists and press against the ties as the big guy cinched his hands. The little wiggle room he gained turned out to be a blessing.

He manages to get one hand half way out. He wriggles around until he is able to sit on his hands for leverage. With determination, he pulls through the pain and yanks it free. Captain Bliss' tiny closet does not have any guns, which he originally hoped he would find. But he rummages around and finds something very interesting. A fiendish smile crosses his face as he picks up an X26 military grade Taser with an extra battery pack, fully charged.

Earlier, he heard Natasha and the other thug enter the room to get Captain Bliss out of the captain's bed, so he is pretty sure he is alone. But he still holds the Taser ready as he kicks the closet door open. Nothing happens. He waits thirty seconds. Seems nobody heard anything. He goes to work on his feet, and with the full use of his hands it only takes a few minutes to work the zip ties off his ankles. He sits down on the captain's bed to think through his next move.

He vividly remembers sitting out on the porch over at Chief Roberto and Isabella's house after his second Bible fellowship. The women were inside and Roberto was elaborating on the section of scripture that was taught earlier.

"You see, it was that Jesus responded to the temptations or attacks of the devil with the written Word of God. That was what backed him down every time."

Chris had said, "Yeah, but then he tempts him with all the kingdoms of the world. What does that mean? "

Roberto had put his hand on Chris' shoulder and said, "The Bible declares that Satan is the god of this world. He wants men and women to worship and serve him, so he bribes them with a kingdom of this world to sell out. In Jesus' case, he pulled out all the stops and offered him everything."

"He didn't take any of it, did he?"

"No, he sure did not. He backed off the god of this world with the Word of the true God. Chris, there are men and women in this world who sell out to all kinds of things for power and glory. We have to resist and sometimes even fight them in many different ways. As Paul said in first Timothy, we fight the good fight. But one thing we always have to remember is that God is our true source of power and deliverance. Without Him there really is never any victory, but when we get Him involved by prayer and believing, we can literally move mountains."

Chris sits there on the bed hardly believing how he just relived that whole experience, but he knows what to do next. He must fight the good fight. He closes his eyes and prays like he has never prayed in his whole life. When he gets up, he knows he can win this thing because he has the most powerful ally there is and they are both ready for action.

*　　*　　*

Danielle stares across the dark waves knowing Captain Bliss and Juan are out there somewhere as they endeavor to maneuver and navigate the sea at night. It's so unfair that all this is happening to her. First her parents and her grandmother; and now her and her grandfather. *God, why is all this happening to me, to us, to my family?* she thinks, questioning God in her mind. She remembers Grandma Isabella telling her about the story of Job in the Bible, how he lost all his wealth and all his children but never blamed God. Finally, when Job prayed for his three friends, God delivered him and blessed him back in double.

Grandpa Jim just asked Boris what's next. She doesn't care that she is in front of all these people in this room, or that they will hear her. Before Boris can answer, she says loud and clear, "God, I let go of my frustration in You for what happened to my parents, and my grandma; I know it was not You. I know that You are a good and gracious God, like Grandpa Roberto has taught me. God, there is nothing too hard for You. Every heart is an open book to You, so I give You the lives of all those children, Captain Bliss, Grandpa Jim, and myself and I thank you for turning this horrible dark time around and saving all our lives in the name of Jesus Christ." A great peace settles into her heart. As the waves carry Juan and the girls away, one word erupts in her heart that is clear, loud, and true; *FIGHT*!

Boris glares at her. He grinds his teeth as his whole face changes into that of a berserk madman. He hates that name. He grabs the blade out of his walking stick, raises it over his head and moves toward Danielle. "There is no Jeezus and no power in the universe that can save you now, you little bitch. You are mine to do with what I want, and I want you dead."

The door to the command deck stairwell bursts open. Chris steps out with the Taser in his right hand. Much to his delight, the closest person is Natasha. He tazes her faster than she can respond with her weapon, which she drops as soon as the fifty thousand volts of electricity shoot through her system.

A whirlwind of activity erupts on the deck of the cruise ship. As Boris heads toward Danielle with that lethal blade and pure murder in his eyes, Jim reaches out, grabs him by the shoulder, whisks him around, and cracks him again in the jaw with a powerful straight right hand. Boris, ready this time, rolls with the punch and brings his right arm around with the blade swinging in a trajectory intending to slice into Jim's neck and shoulder. But Jim is ready with a counter of his own. He throws his left arm up in a c-position just over his forehead and catches Boris' arm in the crook of his arm. He grabs the back of Boris' hand and steps back with his right leg as he twists the blade free from his hand. It lands harmlessly on the deck.

Boris looks up at the caterer and shouts, "What are you staring at you fool? Kill him!" Before the caterer can even move, a large powerful fist smashes into his face. Tom retrieves the thug's Uzi and holds him to the ground with it. The other bad caterer across the deck sees the whole situation going south and raises his gun to respond, but he suddenly feels the cold steel of another Uzi up against his throat as Alyeks shoves it into his neck and says, "Make any move at all and your brains will cover half this ship."

Chris responds to Alyeks' unexpected help, steps over Natasha's unconscious body, and removes the Uzi from the thug caterer's hands.

Danielle can hardly believe the miraculous event she sees transpire before her eyes following her prayer. She quickly rehearses in her mind what just happened.

As Boris closed in to kill her, Grandpa Jim stopped him. At the same time, Chris burst through a door onto the deck and shoots Natasha with something that makes her drop her weapon and fall to the ground convulsing. The event coordinator punches one of Boris' thugs knocking him out, and takes his weapon away. And the most astonishing thing to her is that Alyeks steps up to the engine room thug, puts his gun to the man's neck, and threatens to blow his head off if he tries anything.

She sees Grandpa is still holding Boris in a very nice wrist lock. He uses his other hand to wipe the sweat off his forehead, smiles at Danielle, and says, "Hold on a moment everyone. This ain't over yet."

He brings Boris to his feet. "I owe this bastard a good ass kicking and that is exactly what he is going to get."

Boris' look of bewilderment is profound, but he soon gathers himself and snaps at Jim. "What do you think this is, you ridiculous old fool? Rock Em Sock Em Robots or something? While you were down in Alabama learning how to buff cars, I was a world class assassin. You are not your ridiculous son who beat up bad guys when they made him angry. You are just some ridiculous Manheim recon worker who got lucky and made a few bucks."

Jim throws a very sharp and very fast left jab into Boris' jaw. As he reels from the blow, Jim says, "Who the hell do you think taught the Hero of Cozumel how to fight in the first place, you stupid evil bastard?"

Then, like nothing Danielle, Chris, or anyone on the deck had ever seen except maybe in a Rocky movie, Jim's fists repeatedly fly into Boris' face and body at warp speed. When he is done, Boris is sprawled over the fishing section, out cold.

They all hear a loud scream from the hallway leading to the second banquet room. Danielle realizes the young voice is one of her students and dashes into the hallway with Chris right behind her. She opens the door to a scene that she knows will be in her mind for the rest of her life. There on the floor of the utility room is Renea, a sixteen-year-old girl in her class. Most of her clothes are torn off. Kneeling over her, holding a knife to her throat, is Rev. Billy Whitehall trying to get his pants undone.

Danielle sees red as the blood rushes to her face. A rage she has never experienced before erupts from deep within her soul as she prepares to attack the worthless and horrible creature before her. As she starts to attack, a strong and firm hand pushes her to one side, and a just as enraged, Lt. Chris Rottanelli steps around her, grabs the knife hand of the reverend and twists it so hard the bone snaps instantly. He stands the man up and rams his forehead into Whitehall's nose, shattering it. Next, he pummels the man with a flurry of fists that rivals Jim Edwards' earlier performance with Boris. As Whitehall moans in a half-conscious stupor on the floor, Chris grabs him by the scruff of his neck and drags him out onto the deck. In front of everyone, he pulls him over to the fishing platform, picks him up and throws him into the dark South Texas Ocean.

Danielle stands there not knowing whether to punch his lights out for brushing her aside, or kiss him for what he just did, but one thing is for certain; she is in love with Lt. Chris Rottanelli. She runs back into the hallway to take care of Renea. She finds the girl gathering her clothing and putting some of it back on.

"Are you all right Renea?" Danielle asks as she helps her.

"He did not rape me, if that is what you mean. He was going to just before you stopped him." The tears pour out of the teenager as she clings to Danielle and holds onto her with all her might.

Outside, Jim grabs a life preserver and throws it at the floundering man in the ocean twelve feet below. "You are a fine officer and an even better man, Chris. I don't want to see you forced out of the Coast Guard over this like my son was. Let's get him back in the boat and let the authorities deal with him later."

Chris nods and they work together on the line to pull Billy back in. With the four men on the deck, they hold the others at bay with the weapons they confiscated as they discuss what to do with them. Tom suggests that they make them all trade places with the captives locked in the walk-in cooler.

"That sounds like a good idea to me," says Danielle as she walks out with Renea.

"What are we going to do about the life boat and the children?"

As Jim, Tom, and Chris get Whitehall situated, Yuri, still a bit dazed from the blow to his head, stands by the door that Chris came through from the command deck when he first tazed Natasha. Rubbing his eyes, Yuri does not see Natasha laying there.

"Uncle Boris," he says, shaking his head and trying to clear his vision. "I hope you killed that mule kicking bitch and her grandpa by now. She is someone I never want to see again." As the blur comes into focus, he is beside himself with astonishment at what he sees.

Like a bolt of lightning, Natasha is on her feet. She shoves Yuri into Chris and the event coordinator, and runs up the stairs to the command deck. Boris, also now lucid, yells to Natasha, "Call my yacht! Go to Plan B immediately!"

Chris, Danielle, and Tom all start to go after Natasha. Alyeks yells, "Don't let her turn the engines on again! If she does the boat will catch fire and blow up!"

They pull back and Chris interjects, "I know these engines. I'm going down to find out what they did to them."

Jim says, "It's going to take at least three of us to get these guys safely to the walk-in fridge."

Alyeks offers to go take care of Natasha, but Danielle says no, she will take care of her, then adds, "The rest of you, get these scum into the fridge and get the other caterers out so they can help us get the boat under control."

Without waiting for anyone to object, Danielle dashes through the door and up to the command deck after Natasha. At the top of the stairs by the helm, she finds Natasha on the ship radio talking to someone. "Yes, we are going to Plan B. We do not have time to wait for our friends coming up the coast. Hone in on my signal, but find that lifeboat first and blow it out of the water."

Danielle is standing at the entrance of the doorway, just having heard Natasha order the violent death of her students. "You bitch. You crazy, evil bitch. You were never going to let them live. No witnesses."

Natasha just laughs as she hangs the microphone on the console. "You are such a naive little girl, Danielle. And you come up here without a gun. How convenient. If you want to save the children, I am sure that my father will be willing to call off the attack in exchange for our freedom." As she talks, she inches closer to the engine switch.

Danielle, not fooled, boldly steps up between her and the switch. "Nice try, but by now the rest of your gang are being locked up in the walk-in refrigerator where you had the catering crew. If you pull that switch, you're signing their death warrants. Chris is a trained engineer and he is heading to the engine room to repair your sabotage. As soon as he is done, we are going to go get my students."

Natasha, in a frenzy, lunges at Danielle with both hands to gouge her eyes out. Danielle, on guard, plants a very hard, lunging side kick to Natasha's abdomen which doubles her over to all fours. She moves in to finish her, but Natasha does a shoulder roll to the side, and the momentum carries her to her feet.

"You have extraordinarily powerful legs, little girl. I said I will no longer underestimate you." Natasha then feints with a straight left strike and jumps up and cracks Danielle in the side of the head with a spinning hook kick. Danielle flies to the side and lands against the helm. But before Natasha can recover her balance, Danielle goes low and sweeps her feet out from under her. Natasha lands with a thud on her back. Danielle rolls over next to her on the deck and elbows her once in the face, and twice in the gut, and kip-ups to her feet. Natasha turns over and gets on her hands and knees, coughing and wheezing as she exclaims, "What the hell! Does your whole fucking family get together for the holidays and have MMA contests in the backyard?"

Danielle laughs. "Not quite, but kind of."

Natasha rolls toward Danielle and from the ground throws a hard round kick aimed at Danielle's knee. Danielle catches the move in time by bending her knee enough to protect the joint. She remembers her daddy always told her, "Never let them take your legs." She rolls to the outer deck and stands, leaning on the railing looking out over the side of the boat. She is fully prepared and expecting the next attack.

Natasha, enraged beyond measure, lunges. Danielle catches her, wraps the palm of her hand around the back of Natasha's head and just under her ear, and pulls and twists at the same time which spins Natasha around and slams her into the railing. Danielle steps back as Natasha spins, her back to the rail, and looks at Danielle with pure hatred.

"Enough of this playing," Natasha says as Danielle sizes up her stance, finds her balance points and the weak one. "My father taught me a thousand ways to kill a little bitch like you, and that is what I am going to do; kill you!"

With her right hand forward, Danielle jumps up, draws her left knee into her stomach, whips her head and shoulders around to the left in a full circle, marks the exact spot on Natasha's chest she is aiming for, and bull whips her hips around, catapulting her left foot into that spot. Natasha's body reacts like someone tied a rope around her chest connected to a boat off the side of the yacht that instantly takes off at full speed. She flies into the ocean below.

Danielle calmly grabs a nearby life preserver, leans over to the side of the boat, and throws it at Natasha. "My daddy taught me how to defend myself, Natasha, but lucky for you, I am not a killer and I never will be. Don't you try to come aboard just yet. You can just cool off down there while I go get my students."

Danielle races over to the ship intercom and punches in the engine room. "Chris, have you gotten anywhere with those engines yet?"

"Yes, I have. You can restart it in a minute. I'll tell you when, but unless you can find a trained boat pilot up there, we've got a problem because my makeshift line isn't going to hold unless I stay here to nursemaid it."

Danielle rolls her eyes. "Chris, are you forgetting who my father is? When I was eleven years old, he let me pilot his *Hamilton-class* cutter around South Padre Island more than once."

"Danielle, that is so illegal on so many levels. I forbid you to tell me that story ever again."

"Whatever, boy scout, just get this garbage scow going so we can go get those kids."

Chris smiles. *God, I love that girl!*

"Okay, it's ready. Start her up."

The silhouette of a very dark and sinister yacht appears off the side of their boat where Natasha had been in the water. Through the dim starlit night, Danielle can barely make out Natasha standing on the bow of the strange yacht. Natasha's voice booms over a bullhorn.

"Okay Danielle, fun and games are over. You will return my father and Yuri immediately. Even if you manage to fix up that yacht's engine, it is no match for this one. We can do ninety plus knots and we're loaded with high-tech military grade weaponry. It's over sweetheart, we have won."

Danielle grabs both sides of her head and screams in frustration, but notices something quite amazing happening on the lower deck. Jim and Tom are on the same side of the boat at the cruise ship skeet shooting setup. They are mounting small propane cylinders, normally used for cooking, on the contraption.

Alyeks appears at the top of the stairs and yells to her, "Jim says to take off at his signal! He said you'll know the signal when you hear it."

Chris announces again over the intercom, "Okay, Danielle, you can start the engines."

Jim shouts, "pull!" The little cylinder flies through the air and lands on the deck of Boris' Modified Millennium 140 close to the engine compartment. With one shotgun blast, the whole compartment bursts into flames. Tom launches another cylinder which descends on a bunch of crates on the Millennium's rear deck. Another shotgun blast, and a huge series of explosions erupts from the crates and lights up the night sky.

Jim looks to see if Danielle got the signal. She did. The yacht starts to pull away at top speed. She knew that Grandpa had won some skeet shooting contests a few years ago when he and Jacob were doing it as a hobby, but she had no idea how expert he was. It thrilled her to see him put it to good use now.

She remains at the helm speeding in the direction in which she saw Bliss tell Juan to pilot the lifeboat. Jim and Tom arrive on the command deck with one of the newly released good-guy caterers.

Jim says, "I don't know how long that will hold them, but I do think it bought us some precious time. Tom just activated the emergency beacon on board, which any Coast Guard or Navy craft should pick up on right away. He is going to stay on the radio here until someone answers. Our cell phones are still useless, probably jammed from somewhere on the ship."

Danielle asks, "How far from Brazos are we now, does anyone know?"

"Probably about forty-five minutes at top speed," Tom says.

"That was some pretty quick thinking down there, Grandpa," Danielle says as she hugs and kisses him on the cheek.

Jim hugs her back. "It was Tom's idea. He's an old sea dog with twenty years in the Navy. He recognized those crates on deck as ammo crates and knew exactly where the engine opening on that thing is too. Heck, he's the skeet shoot operator for this boat. He says he's gotten so good at aiming that shooter he could probably take a seagull down with it."

Danielle peers straight out and sees the little lifeboat just at the crest of her vision. "There they are!" She maneuvers the yacht alongside the boat so it is next to the ladder by the fishing stand. It takes three men to get Captain Bliss back on board. Tom tells everyone that he is the boat's emergency medical officer and a licensed EMT in Houston when he is not out on the yacht. They help him get Bliss to his cabin where he can properly assess the damage Natasha did to him, and begin some treatment.

Juan helps the other girls back on board as they all clamor that Renea is not with them. "I am okay," Renea says as she steps out of the door from the banquet room.

Juan runs up and hugs and kisses her, but then just as quickly pulls back as he realizes everyone is watching him. The little girls start to giggle.

After a few minutes cruising at top speed, Chris yells over the intercom to turn off the engines because the line just blew again. He estimates about ten minutes to repair it. Danielle cuts the engines and the *Princess Royale II* slows to drift, bobbing silently out at sea.

CHAPTER TWELVE
HELL OF A NIGHT

***Princess Royale II*, Drifting at Sea**

Danielle nervously checks the time, then tells her grandfather they better grab any weapon they can find and prepare to defend themselves because Boris' yacht is going to be there any minute to rescue him and Yuri. Within seconds they all look out and see it coming at an unbelievable speed.

But something else phenomenal happens. Two more ships appear, one on each side of the approaching yacht, perpendicular to it. A Coast Guard patrol cutter comes from the north, and the other, a Mexican Interceptor, comes from the south. As the two boats race toward the scene, the modified Millennium makes a hard turn toward the smaller Mexican Interceptor, does a complete one-eighty, and heads out to sea at what everyone thinks has to be close to 100 knots.

Jim says to Alyeks, "Go tell Chris that he is about to be rescued by his own boat."

Within minutes, both boats are lined up on either side of the *Princess Royale II*, and a delegation from each ship climbs aboard, consisting of Chris' second-in-command Wallace, Ranger Major John Brown, Deputy Director Chuck Yeager, Captain Larry Phillips, Captain Marnia Gonzalez, and a few others.

Chuck makes notes and does some preliminary debriefing of Yuri's and Boris' former captives. Marnia's men arrest and move Yuri over to her boat, and a dispute erupts over who should take Boris into custody. Marnia holds her ground, even though she is quite outnumbered by all the representatives of the United States government.

"Gentlemen, I believe it is in all of our best interests that I take Boris into custody and let my people interrogate and hold him. After all, if he is truly The Chameleon, then he is wanted in my country and several other South American countries as well. But there is no warrant for such a person in the United States. In fact, outside of the incident on this boat, and the eye witnesses you have here, all you have to hold him on is circumstantial at best. Let's be honest, if he is guilty of half the things we suspect he is, and has not been caught or detained yet, what makes you think you can hold him with your...how shall I say it...your 'criminal friendly judicial system'?"

Yeager pipes in. "Now, you wait just a minute Marnia. We had an agreement."

Major Brown adds, "Chuck, she's making a lot of sense to me. If this guy is half as connected as you say he is, he'll be out on bail in no time and then he'll disappear."

Marnia feels the old Ranger just gave her the upper hand. "Listen gentleman. I will take him back to my country and introduce him to our press as the man responsible for the death of the Hero of Cozumel. That alone should ensure that he will not be going anywhere too soon."

Jim Edwards adds his two cents. "I vote for the young *señorita* here. Oh, and by the way, thanks for all the Christmas and birthday cards over the years."

The Coast Guard officers bring Boris out of the cooler and on to the deck. He refuses to look at anyone. Across the deck over on the Mexican Interceptor, Yuri yells, "I want to make a deal! You're going to pin everything on me. It was all my uncle Boris. I will tell you everything I know. I will show you all his secrets in the United States, please!"

Boris rams his head into the nose of one of the men escorting him, knees the other in the groin, and lunges over to the fishing stand to grab the harpoon gun before anyone can react to stop him. He aims it at Yuri and spears him through heart from ten yards away, killing him instantly.

Brown and Yeager both tackle Boris and put him face down on the deck. Brown takes his handcuffs and locks Boris' hands behind his back. They stand him up.

Chuck says to Marnia, "I guess that determines who Boris is going with. He just killed a man in United States jurisdiction."

Captain Phillips clears his throat and says, "Ah, excuse me, I don't know if anyone has noticed, but we have actually drifted into Mexican waters."

Having heard enough of everything, and after a harrowing night, Jim gets more than a little irritated with all the squabbling. He steps over, grabs Boris by his collar and handcuffs, force-walks him to the side of the boat where the Mexican Interceptor sits, and says, "Marnia, tell your boys over there to catch." He lifts Boris, swings him and heaves him over the rail onto the Mexican Polaris Interceptor. With a big smile he says, "Nice arrest honey. Now go bury that piece of garbage where no one will ever find him again."

Despite herself, Marnia can't stop her heart from fluttering. There is just something about these Edwards men that reminds her of John Wayne. "Thank you, Jim. We will do just that."

Two Mexican military men yank Boris to his feet to escort him away. As they spin him around, he sees something that he cannot fathom or accept. Climbing up the ladder onto the yacht coming from the Coast Guard cutter are Roberto and Isabella Garcia. He completely loses it, and like a possessed wildman, thrashing and wailing, he attempts to get back on the yacht with his hands still cuffed behind his back and two men struggling to hold him. He kicks, writhes, tries to bite his captors, and screams, "That's impossible! They're dead! They're dead!"

Marnia's men use a handheld Taser to subdue him and take him below deck.

Chuck is still a little indignant about the Mexicans getting Boris, but he knows when the odds are stacked against him, so he concedes. They hear a loud foghorn and turn to see a very large and impressive United States Coast Guard security cutter about a hundred yards away. From a deafening loudspeaker, a voice booms over the waters. "This is Captain Maelstrom of the United States Coast Guard. We would have been here sooner, but we had a knockdown drag-out with some pirates farther south in very well armed cutter that was headed this way. Standby, we will meet up with you shortly."

While Maelstrom's security cutter makes its way to the side of the yacht, and before getting on Chris' waiting cutter, Jim grabs Boris' watertight briefcase containing all that paperwork he was going to use to take over his company.

"Is that something I need to be concerned about, Mister Edwards?" Chuck asks. Jim smiles and says, "Probably, but I want my lawyers to look at it first if you don't mind." Chuck leaves it at that figuring Jim has had a hell of a night.

*　　*　　*

After a brief meeting at Station Brazos with United States and Mexican law enforcement and Coast Guard people, everyone heads in different directions.

Danielle runs up to Alyeks and says, "You really surprised me back there Alyeks, we would all probably be dead if you had not switched sides. I'm sorry I flipped you off."

Alyeks gives an exasperated sigh and puts a hand on her shoulder, "Danielle, I have never been on Boris' side. I have been his slave for many years. It would appear that has changed, and I have some big decisions ahead of me, but some things are for certain."

Danielle can't help but ask, "What would those things be, Alyeks?"

Alyeks is very serious when he says, "I don't know if it would be safe for me to return to Russia. Natasha is still out there; also, I absolutely need to find my brother here in the United States to protect him; and finally, I really want to see your extraordinary children dance. We almost lost our lives together and I want to honor their courage."

Chuck pipes in, "I think that the FBI can help you with finding your brother, but the dancing part is totally up to Danielle."

Danielle gives Alyeks an affectionate hug. "I think that dancing for you is exactly what we should do. I will call you tomorrow."

Captain Larry Phillips comes walking out of the main building at Station Brazos and practically runs into Barbara, who is standing on the dock saying goodbye to her friend Marnia Gonzalez. The beautiful Honduran woman leaves the Corpus Christi Sector Commander stammering as he endeavors to introduce himself. Marnia jumps in to help the poor captain out as she introduces them to each other. She is not surprised at the captain's reaction to Barbara, but is very intrigued to see that Barbara is impacted by the captain's presence as well. Marnia boards her boat and thinks to herself, *maybe there is some true happiness in store for Barbara out of all this. That would sure be something.*

CHAPTER THIRTEEN
NEW REVELATIONS

One Week Later, Saturday Night

The recital had been canceled for a variety of obvious reasons but by Alyeks' urging was rescheduled for the following weekend. Captain Bliss was taken to the emergency room at a local hospital where he was diagnosed with a concussion and puncture wound below his right collarbone. He was released in four days, went to Roberto and Isabella's house to visit with them and Danielle, and went home to Houston. Major John Brown arrested Rev. Billy Whitehall after Jim gave him some pictures they found in the papers Boris left behind, depicting Billy and an underage girl in his congregation having sexual relations. After the arrest, a couple of other families came forward citing rape and sexual harassment by the pastor.

Captain Marnia Gonzalez brought Boris back to Mexico City and charged him with a myriad of crimes against the country, as well as the murder of a United States citizen in Mexican waters. After she let it leak out that Boris is the one who had the Hero of Cozumel and his family killed, several assassination attempts were made by other prisoners. They had to move him to a more secure location pending state trial.

Danielle and Chris got to spend a good deal of time together because the Coast Guard gave Chris the week off and Roberto insisted Danielle take a break. So they spent most of the week in the dance studio hanging out with each other. By the time Saturday night came around, she felt that everybody was ready for the recital. She was so relieved that Billy Whitehall had not defiled Renea and was more than a little surprised at how far Renea and Juan's budding romance had progressed since the yacht incident.

*   *   *

Danielle stands at the side of the stage in the Boys Club Community Center where Juan does his boxing training. She is a little surprised to see almost all the boys from the local boxing team sitting in the audience. She also sees her grandpas standing at the back. Her grandmother is in the front row next to Alyeks. With Alyeks being there and with all the drama of the prior weekend, the local news station has a reporter from their Houston office covering the story and the recital. Danielle is on edge. She never got this nervous when she had to dance before, not even in Philadelphia at Temple. But she's definitely battling some major butterflies tonight.

The recital is a four-part performance depicting a struggling family in poverty. The father is trying to start a new fishing business, but everyone in the village ridicules his idea. In the end, his whole family stands by him and is able to succeed with their help. Danielle wrote, directed, and choreographed the whole thing herself, and the children did extraordinarily well.

Every time Danielle looks out at Alyeks, he is completely unreadable, which really makes her butterflies go berserk. The last scene, her favorite, she titled, *"Stand by You"* which ended with the finale that she choreographed to the song by Rachel Platten with the same title. She really loves Juan's performance in this act and wants to get the full impact, so she goes to the back and stands with her grandpas to watch it.

Besides, she has something very important she wants to discuss with both of them right after the show and she wants to make sure they keep themselves available. As the fourth section starts, she looks over at Jim and sees that he is visibly shaken and sobbing. She and Roberto help him into the lobby where the three of them can be alone for a few minutes.

"Grandpa, what is wrong?"

Jim wipes his eyes and looks at his granddaughter with pure love. "I'm sorry, Danielle. That performance just reminded me of why I love the business so much. You see, your grandmother and I founded that place together. We always wanted your dad to have it someday. It's just that it's a family business, and now, there is no family there. I guess what I am trying to say is if I can't do it with someone, I don't want it anymore."

Danielle takes both of her grandfather's hands in hers, looks them in the eyes, and tenderly says, "Grandpas, that's what I wanted to talk to both of you about. I want to come home now. I am ready to step into Daddy's shoes and run Edwards Auto with you. You don't have to do it alone anymore."

Jim hardly believes what he is hearing. "Are you really sure, honey? Really, really sure?"

Danielle laughs and grabs Jim to give him a big hug. "Yes, Grandpa, I am really, really, sure!"

They hear the music and know that the grand finale is about to start, so the three of them go back in to see Juan and Renea do their final routine. When it is done and the children stop, there is complete silence in the room for an unbelievably long five seconds, then everyone gets on their feet and gives a thunderous applause with loud cheers of excitement. To everyone's amazement, Alyeks of the Russian Ballet Academy walks up onto to the stage and over to Juan and Renea, grabs both their hands, and thrusts them up in the air yelling "Bravo! Bravo!" as tears stream down his face.

Jim looks over at Danielle. "Does he always do stuff like that?"

Danielle, visibly shocked, looks back at her grandfather. "I don't think he has ever done that for anyone ever before. When he came to Temple for our recital, he could barely remember what dance anyone did, and he didn't know anyone's names or what parts they had."

About an hour later, everyone is outside the community center saying goodbye to children as they meet their parents in the lobby to leave. Alyeks stands next to Danielle, her grandfathers, and Isabella, shaking peoples' hands and complimenting all the children for each one of their parts, even remembering and noting details about each child's performance.

After a while, Alyeks looks over at Danielle and says, "Danielle Edwards, I was wrong about you. You have a rare gift in teaching and cultivating passion. These children, though in need of some technical instruction, have a passion and pure love for dance that I have not seen very much in a long time. You have somehow tapped into it beautifully."

Danielle, blown away by Alyeks' words, manages to say "thank you" before she too chokes up.

"My wife and I have been talking about moving to the United States someday. Now that I am getting out from under Boris' yoke, I would like to expedite that ambition as quickly as possible."

Danielle is a little taken aback that Alyeks is married and asks him about it.

"I thought you knew? My wife is Patti, your former roommate from the university in Philadelphia."

"You married Patti?" Danielle turns around and exclaims, "I was so mad at her when she dropped that contract with the New York Dance Company and ran off to go study under the Great Alyeks Yeshlton. I have not heard from her in almost three years."

Alyeks clears his throat and tells Danielle that Patti did mention something about Danielle's abhorrence to her running after an older man like that. "We have been very happily married for about two years now, but have kept it very quiet to not draw the attention of people like Boris. Now I want to bring Patti home, search for my brother, and perhaps assist you here with these prodigies you are teaching."

Danielle laughs. "Alyeks, I'm sorry, but this is a not-for-profit school here. What the studio is allowed to pay me does not even cover my rent, and I live in an efficiency."

"Danielle," Alyeks says, "my love for the art has never had anything to do with money, and because of our past mutual friend Boris, I will never want for money in my life. What I want is to experience what we just did, in this…how do you say… 'community center'—pure art, pure passion."

Juan and Renea walk out together, and Juan hurries over to Danielle to say, "I am glad you are still here because I want you to see this." He points to the circle drive, and pulling in is Juan's dad Miguel in the '67

Mustang they all restored—all put back together and looking very fine.

Jim and Roberto are awed by the spectacular automobile before them, but it is Alyeks who is completely flabbergasted at what he sees pulling in.

"Is this a 1967 Ford Mustang Fastback convertible?" he says as he goes out to behold the beauty, examining every square inch of the automotive wonder before him.

Danielle tells him that it is indeed that, and has been completely restored with stock parts and should qualify for a classic rating.

Alyeks looks at Juan. "How much do you want? I will pay any price. I must have this car. It is for sale, is it not?"

Juan looks at his dad, who in turns looks at Danielle. Just as she is about to speak, Jim Edwards says, "I will give you forty-five thousand dollars for it right now."

Danielle looks at Miguel and says, "See, I told you. There is Juan's college tuition room and board for the first two years."

Alyeks looks at Miguel. "If you are selling this to pay for this prodigy's college, I will give you one hundred thousand dollars for this car right now."

A flabbergasted Jim says, "Are you out of your mind? You can buy two or three—ouch!" Danielle elbows her grandpa in the stomach and gives him a big shush. Jim is a bit shocked, but then gets it and says to Alyeks, "You have bought yourself a fine piece of great American automotive history, young man. Enjoy."

Chris joins them and asks Danielle, "Did you tell him yet?" Danielle puts herself under Chris' arm, wraps her arm around his waist, and nods in the affirmative.

Jim looks down at the couple and says, "You know Danielle, Yuri and Boris have left a real mess down here for Edwards Auto to clean up, and you know I don't like leaving HQ that much. I have been thinking, maybe the new vice president can come down here once or twice a month for a while just to clean things up. I'll let you use that minor in international business law you were so excited about. What do you think about that idea?"

Danielle and Chris are almost giggling when she replies, "Why, I think that is an excellent idea, Grandpa."

Later that week, Alyeks contacts Danielle to let her know the FBI located his brother in Dallas, Texas at a very good cancer center and he is responding nicely to treatment. Danielle is ecstatic to hear that Alyeks and Patti are serious about coming to South Texas to teach dance at her not-for-profit center. She lets him know that she is moving back to Pennsylvania to help her grandfather run Edwards Auto, but that the board of directors of the dance studio would fall all over themselves to have Alyeks run the whole thing. Alyeks assures Danielle that he would not have it any other way, unless she wanted to stay of course.

One Month Later, Thursday Evening, Edwards Auto

Danielle is still getting used to sitting at her daddy's desk. She refuses to change anything about the office. It now brings back positive and wonderful memories of her mom and dad. Grandpa is out in the detail shop helping with final inspection, and she is finishing up on car registrations for tomorrow's sale. She is just about done when she hears a tap on the door and yells, "Come in!"

The door opens and in walks Captain Marnia Gonzalez and Deputy Director Chuck Yeager.

Danielle jumps up and exclaims, "Chuck, Marnia! What brings you guys to Manheim? Come on in and sit down. How can I help you?"

Chuck is the first to speak. "Danielle, you'd better sit down. We have something very serious to tell you and Jim, but we thought we should tell you first so you can help us break it to Jim."

Danielle is trying to control her emotions as she asks the duo what is going on.

Marnia intensely looks at Danielle and says, "Danielle. Your father, your mother, and your grandmother are still alive."